Three Against One

Before Clint reached the three rustlers, he knew they'd go for their guns. He tried to cut them off before they did it.

"Take it easy, boys," he called out. "Nobody needs to get hurt."

"What do we do?" Dutch Louie hissed at his two partners.

"Run!" Bill Williams said. "That's got to be Clint Adams."

"We have to fight," Orville said. "If we don't, Jack will kill us."

Clint reined his horse in, looked down at the three men.

"The easy way to do this is for you to lay down your guns."

Williams wanted to run, but if Louie and Orville survived, they'd mark him as a coward.

"Come on," Clint said. "Nobody has to die."

"Wrong!" a panicked Swift Bill said. "You do."

He went for his gun . . .

DON'T MISS THESE ALL-ACTION WESTERN SERIES FROM THE BERKLEY PUBLISHING GROUP

THE GUNSMITH by J. R. Roberts

Clint Adams was a legend among lawmen, outlaws, and ladies. They called him . . . the Gunsmith.

LONGARM by Tabor Evans

The popular long-running series about Deputy U.S. Marshal Custis Long—his life, his loves, his fight for justice.

SLOCUM by Jake Logan

Today's longest-running action Western. John Slocum rides a deadly trail of hot blood and cold steel.

BUSHWHACKERS by B. J. Lanagan

An action-packed series by the creators of Longarm! The rousing adventures of the most brutal gang of cutthroats ever assembled—Quantrill's Raiders.

DIAMONDBACK by Guy Brewer

Dex Yancey is Diamondback, a Southern gentleman turned con man when his brother cheats him out of the family fortune. Ladies love him. Gamblers hate him. But nobody pulls one over on Dex . . .

WILDGUN by Jack Hanson

The blazing adventures of mountain man Will Barlow—from the creators of Longarm!

TEXAS TRACKER by Tom Calhoun

J.T. Law: the most relentless—and dangerous—manhunter in all Texas. Where sheriffs and posses fail, he's the best man to bring in the most vicious outlaws—for a price

J. R. ROBERTS

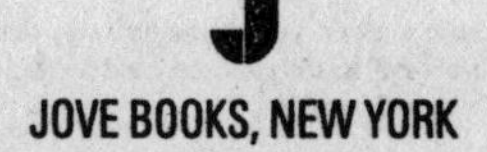

JOVE BOOKS, NEW YORK

THE BERKLEY PUBLISHING GROUP
Published by the Penguin Group
Penguin Group (USA) Inc.
375 Hudson Street, New York, New York 10014, USA
Penguin Group (Canada), 90 Eglinton Avenue East, Suite 700, Toronto, Ontario M4P 2Y3, Canada
(a division of Pearson Penguin Canada Inc.)
Penguin Books Ltd., 80 Strand, London WC2R 0RL, England
Penguin Group Ireland, 25 St. Stephen's Green, Dublin 2, Ireland (a division of Penguin Books Ltd.)
Penguin Group (Australia), 250 Camberwell Road, Camberwell, Victoria 3124, Australia
(a division of Pearson Australia Group Pty. Ltd.)
Penguin Books India Pvt. Ltd., 11 Community Centre, Panchsheel Park, New Delhi—110 017, India
Penguin Group (NZ), 67 Apollo Drive, Rosedale, Auckland 0632, New Zealand
(a division of Pearson New Zealand Ltd.)
Penguin Books (South Africa) (Pty.) Ltd., 24 Sturdee Avenue, Rosebank, Johannesburg 2196,
South Africa

Penguin Books Ltd., Registered Offices: 80 Strand, London WC2R 0RL, England

BITTERROOT VALLEY

A Jove Book / published by arrangement with the author

PRINTING HISTORY
Jove edition / July 2011

ISBN: 978-0-515-14964-7

JOVE®
Jove Books are published by The Berkley Publishing Group,
a division of Penguin Group (USA) Inc.,
375 Hudson Street, New York, New York 10014.
JOVE® is a registered trademark of Penguin Group (USA) Inc.
The "J" design is a trademark of Penguin Group (USA) Inc.

PRINTED IN THE UNITED STATES OF AMERICA

10 9 8 7 6 5 4 3 2 1

ONE

Clint Adams rode into the Montana's Bitterroot Valley at the behest of his friend, Nathan Piven. Piven was the sheriff of Judith Gap, located about fifty miles south of the Judith Basin. It was also about two hundred miles due east of Helena.

Clint didn't know yet what the fuss was, but he knew when he got a telegram from a friend who was a lawman, there wasn't a fuss far behind.

Judith Gap was a small town, but the lawman there held sway over much of the land that ran along the Musselshell River. That included the Judith Gap, where Clint knew many of the largest ranches in the area were located. His guess was that there was some rustling going on. But Nat Piven would have been able to handle a normal case of rustling without much help. Clint stopped trying to guess, decided to wait to hear the news right from the horse's mouth.

* * *

His name was Stringer Jack. That was the only name anyone knew him by. His men respected him, did everything he told them to do. Riding with him, as always, were Paddy Rose, Swift Bill, Dixie Burr, Orville Edwards, and Silas Nickerson.

They were staying in a tent between the banks of the Musselshell River and a cabin where Old Man James lived in an area known as Bates Point. James was an old-time rustler who'd gotten out of the business, but didn't mind supplying shelter for those who were still active. He lived there with his two boys, who wanted to ride with Stringer Jack but had not yet done so.

Jack came out of the tent and accepted a cup of coffee handed to him by Dixie.

"Me and the boys been wonderin' . . ." Dixie said.

"Wondering what?"

"When we wuz gonna hit the DHS."

The DHS Ranch was the biggest ranch in the area, owned and run by Granville Stewart.

"We'll get to it," Jack said. "You know once we hit him, Stewart's gonna come lookin' for us."

"What do we care?" Dixie asked. "We ain't afraid of him . . . are we?"

"No," Stringer Jack said. "We're not afraid of him, Dixie. Look, get breakfast going and get the rest of the boys up. I'm gonna go talk to Old Man James."

"Yeah, okay, boss."

Jack refilled his cup, then carried it up to the Old Man James's cabin.

Granville Stewart came out onto his veranda, holding a cup of coffee. He looked out over his sprawling ranch in the Judith Basin. From where he was, he could see thousands of head of cattle. And his corral was overcrowded with horses.

Rustlers had been working the area, but so far had not hit him. If and when they did, they would be in trouble.

Stewart was leaving for Helena today, to discuss the situation with some of the other cattlemen in the area. He knew they were going to try to get him to take an active role in tracking down the rustlers, but he wasn't ready to. He would, however, go and listen.

A meeting of cattlemen in Helena would not be worth the time unless Granville Stewart was attending.

Clint rode into Judith Gap, which he found to be a small but bustling town. He dropped Eclipse off at the livery, made his way to the nearest hotel and checked in, then went looking for Nat Piven.

He located the sheriff's office, entered without knocking. Piven turned from the gun rack, where he was returning a shotgun, and grinned broadly.

"Clint, goddamit!" he shouted. "You made it."

Piven was a big man in his forties with a booming voice and a bone-crushing handshake.

"Hey, Nat," Clint said. "Well, you asked me to come so, yeah, I made it."

"Just get in?"

"Took care of my horse, got a room, and came to see you. Haven't even brushed the dust off."

"You hungry?"

"Starving and thirsty."

He slapped Clint on the back and said, "Come on, I'll buy you a steak and a beer."

"Any good?"

"Best in Montana."

"The steak or the beer?"

"Both!"

TWO

Stringer Jack passed the bottle back to Old Man James, who accepted it and drank deeply.

"So what're you gonna do?" the old man asked.

"I hear the cattlemen are meetin' in Helena," Jack said.

"Yeah, so?"

"I'm thinkin' this might be the time to hit 'em and hit 'em hard."

"You talkin' about hittin' the DHS?"

"Yep," Jack said.

"Granville Stewart?"

"Why not?"

"You know," the old man said, "there's plenty of ranches you can rustle cattle and horses from and make a nice livin' for you and your boys. Why take on that kinda trouble?"

Jack took the bottle back.

"What's the point of doin' somethin' if you're only gonna do it halfway?" he asked.

Old Man James took a deep breath and said, "Well, I guess it's up to you, boy."

"Yeah," Jack said. "It's up to me."

He upended the bottle and emptied it.

They caught up on five years while they ate their steak and drank their first beer. Over the second beer, Piven told Clint why he'd asked him to come.

"Rustlers," he said. "Been raiding ranches all along the Musselshell for months."

"What do the cattlemen have to say?"

"They do a lot of talking, but they aren't taking much action. They're pushing me to stop it."

"Rustlers do anything yet but rustle?"

"You mean murder? No, not yet. If they had, I might be able to get some help."

"No deputies?"

"The town doesn't have enough money."

"Wait," Clint said, "they want you to keep the law along the Musselshell . . . alone?"

"That's it."

"What about a posse?"

"By the time I hear about the rustling, and get a posse together, there's nobody to chase."

"What about tracking?"

"You know how many cattle there are around here? The entire basin is covered with tracks. How do I know which tracks were left by rustled cattle?"

"Then what can I do to help?"

"I'm not sure," Piven said, "but I knew I needed help, and you were the one I thought of."

"Well, tell me what's going on."

"The cattlemen are meetin' this week in Helena," the lawman said. "I think they finally got Granville Stewart to agree to attend."

"Stewart?"

"He has the biggest spread in the Basin."

"Has he been hit by the rustlers?"

"Not yet."

"I wonder why."

"I wonder, too."

Clint tried to pay for the meal but Piven told him that in the absence of a deputy he got free meals.

"That includes you."

They left the restaurant, stopped on the boardwalk outside.

"Let's go to Helena," Clint said.

"What?"

"Well, the cattlemen are having a meeting, right?" Clint asked. "Let's go to the meeting."

"We'd have to check in with the sheriff there when we arrive."

"That's no problem."

"I've got nobody to leave in charge here," Piven said. "If the rustlers hit while I'm in Montana—"

"Okay, say no more," Clint said. "I'll go to Montana, meet Granville Stewart, maybe talk to some of the other cattlemen . . ."

"You won't have official standing."

"Believe me, that won't be a problem."

Clint knew that his name alone would get him into the Cattleman's Club in Helena, and that they'd probably want to try and use him.

"Clint . . . you just got here. Now you're gonna ride two hundred miles to Helena?"

"Two hundred miles by stage," Clint said, "won't be the same as two hundred miles for me and Eclipse."

"At least get some sleep and leave in the morning. They're not meeting for three days."

"Okay, I'll do that," Clint said. "I could use a bath and a bed."

"Why don't you get that bath," Piven said, "and I'll meet you at the saloon later for a beer."

"Which saloon?"

"Honey's," Piven said. "Honey's Saloon, down the street."

"Okay," Clint said. "I'll see you there tonight, then."

"After eight," Piven said. "I usually finish my rounds with a beer there."

"See you then."

They walked in separate directions.

The hotel had bath facilities, which Clint availed himself of. He went to his room and, while wearing clean clothes, took the opportunity to clean the trail dust off his boots. Why, he didn't know, since by the time he got to Helena, he'd be covered again.

He considered taking the stage to Helena, decided against it, then wondered how Granville Stewart was going to get there.

He pulled his boots on and left the hotel to go over to Honey's Saloon.

THREE

Clint was standing at the bar in Honey's Saloon when Sheriff Nat Piven came through the batwings. He quickly ordered the lawman a beer before he got to the bar. And he paid for it.

"On me," Clint said. "You can get the next one."

"How do you like this place?" he asked.

Clint looked around. Seemed a fairly typical setup, except for the painting over the bar.

"Why's that there?" he asked.

"That," Piven said, "is Honey."

Clint looked up at the oil painting of a cow.

"The saloon is named after a cow?"

"Apparently," the lawman said, "that cow meant a lot to the owner."

"Well, I've seen saloons named after lots of things. Why not a cow?"

"Why not?"

The saloon was busy, most of the tables taken, a

couple of poker games going, three girls working the floor, and two bartenders behind the bar.

There were only one or two spaces left at the bar, but Clint and the law were given a wide berth, so they were able to stand comfortably.

"I have a question."

"Shoot," Piven said.

"Granville Stewart," Clint said. "How is he getting to Helena?"

"He's leavin' on tomorrow's stage. Why?"

"Well, I was thinking of riding there myself, but now I'm wondering if I should take the stage, get to know the big man along the way."

"Would you let him know who you are and why you're goin' there?"

"I'll tell him who I am," Clint said, "but there's no need to tell him any more. I'll surprise him by showing up at the Cattleman's Club. By the way, how do I get in?"

"I'll send word ahead by telegram," Piven said. "You won't have a problem. Stop in and see Sheriff Dan Lewis. He'll get you in."

"That's good. Anybody I should know about on that end?"

"Naw," Piven said. "You'll meet them all when you get there. They're just ranchers. Stewart's the strongest of the bunch."

"They want him to take an active role, right?"

"Yup."

"Why wouldn't he?"

"I think he would," Piven said, "but he'd wanna be in charge. I think when he does move, it'll be on his own."

"Not with the law?"

"I guess we'll have to see. Once he finds out who you are, he might try to hire you right there in the stagecoach."

"Not likely if there are other passengers."

"Oh, there will be," Piven said. "There always are. The stage to Helena is usually full."

"Then maybe it'll be an interesting ride," Clint said. "Can you get me on there in the morning, with no ticket?"

"Leave it to me," Piven said. "I'll get to the stage office nice and early and arrange it."

"Good. I'll get some rest, then."

"Why?" Piven asked. "You can rest on the stage. Why don't you play some poker?"

"With those men?" Clint asked, pointing. "Please. They wouldn't keep me awake."

He finished his beer and set the mug down on the bar.

"I'll see you in the morning."

Clint went back to his room, spent time cleaning his pistol and rifle, making sure they were in perfect working order. There was no doubt he was going to be hunting rustlers. His weapons and his horse all had to be ready.

After that, he did some reading, settling for a copy of the local newspaper since he didn't have a book with him this time. He was anxiously awaiting a new Mark Twain book.

There were some stories about the rustling, but nowhere did he see the name of any suspected rustlers. Piven hadn't mentioned any either. He wondered if his friend even had any suspects in mind.

Before going to bed, Clint stuck a chair under the doorknob. His window didn't open onto a roof or balcony, so he didn't worry about it. If there were any rustlers in the area and they heard he was in town, they might assume he'd been called in for them. He didn't need any surprises in the middle of the night.

Fairly secure, he turned in early. He was going to need to make arrangements for Eclipse to be cared for in the morning, before he got on the stage. He'd probably be gone several days.

He went to sleep thinking he pretty much knew what lay ahead.

FOUR

Clint went to the livery before doing anything else in the morning. He paid in advance for the liveryman to watch over Eclipse.

"He better be in good shape when I get back," he warned.

"Don't worry, mister," the man said. "A horse like that deserves the best care I can give 'im."

After that, he went to the stage station to make sure Sheriff Piven had arranged for his passage.

"Sure thing," the clerk said. "Got your ticket right here, Mister Adams."

It was clear from the way he said the name that he knew who Clint was.

"Thanks," Clint said. "Where can I get some breakfast?"

"Place across the street is pretty good," the clerk said. "There's already some other passengers over there eatin'."

"Thanks."

He stuck his ticket in his shirt pocket and walked across the street.

Granville Stewart was sitting at a table alone. His foreman had brought him to town, let him off at the station. He'd taken this stage many times before, knew that the breakfast across the street was decent. Except for an occasional business dinner, these were the only times he ate in town.

Across the floor from him he saw Evie Loomis, the reporter for the local paper, *The Judith Page*. It was obvious why she was going to Helena. When she looked over at him, he raised his coffee cup to her in greeting, but she ignored him. Too bad. She was a lovely thing, even if she was twenty years younger than he was.

At fifty, Stewart was fit as ever, spent many days in the saddle, riding the range alongside his men. And if it came down to it, and there were rustlers to track down, he'd be in the saddle doing that, too.

Evie Loomis watched Granville Stewart lift his cup to her and looked away. She was going to Helena to cover the meeting of the cattlemen, knew she'd have to interview him when she got there, but that didn't mean she had to speak to him, or acknowledge his presence, now or in the stage.

She was seated with a middle-aged married couple who were also traveling to Helena. They had met in the station and decided to have breakfast together.

"That well-dressed, handsome man is saluting you with his cup, dear," the woman said.

"That well-dressed man is an ass," Evie said. "Excuse my language."

The woman blushed, but the man just laughed and shook his head.

At that point a man entered the café, with a stage ticket sticking out of his pocket.

"Now that's a handsome man," Evie said.

The other woman looked and said, "Perhaps, but not nearly as well dressed."

"Oh my God," Evie said.

"What is it, my dear?" the man asked.

"I think I know who that is."

"Who?" both husband and wife asked.

But she didn't answer. She just watched him walk across the room and sit at a table.

"Excuse me," she said to the couple. She took her plate and her coffee and carried them over to the man's table.

"May I join you?"

FIVE

Clint looked up at the woman.

"If you can tell me something good to order, sure," he said.

"I have eggs and bacon," she said. "And biscuits. They're very good."

A middle-aged waitress came over.

"Scrambled eggs, bacon, and biscuits, please," he said. "And coffee."

"Comin' up."

She left. Clint looked up at the woman standing there holding her plate and cup.

"Sit down," he invited.

"Thank you."

She sat across from him. Thirties, pretty face, freckles.

"What's your name?" he asked.

"Evie. Evie Loomis."

"Hello, Evie Loomis. What can I do for you?"

"You're Clint Adams."

"How do you know that?"

"I saw you once," she said. "In Denver."

"What were you doing in Denver once?"

"Trying to get a job."

"And you ended up here?"

She nodded.

"I kept tryin' to get a job until I got here," she said. "Then I got hired."

"As what?"

"I'm a reporter," she said. "I work for *The Judith Page*."

"I see."

"Why were you in Judith?" she asked. "Why are you going to Helena?"

"Are you trying to interview me?"

"I'm just curious," she said.

"So this isn't an interview?"

"No," she said. "If it was, I'd have some paper to write on."

"Then why all the questions?"

"I told you, I'm curious."

"Are you going to Helena, or do you just like the food here?" he asked.

"I'm going to Helena," she said. "To cover the meeting of the cattlemen there."

"Then you know who Granville Stewart is," he said.

"Unfortunately, I do."

"Why unfortunately?"

"I don't like him."

"Would you point him out to me?"

"Sure," she said. "Two tables up on your right. He's probably looking at me."

"You're right," Clint said, "he is."

The waitress came over, put Clint's breakfast down in front of him.

"Thank you."

"Sure, sweetie."

Clint started eating his breakfast and stopped talking.

"How is it?" Evie asked.

"It's very good," he said.

"See? I don't lie."

"You must not be very good at your job, then."

"Why do you say that?"

"Because I never met a newspaper reporter who didn't lie."

"Is that so?" she asked. "Maybe I can get better at my job."

"Maybe you can."

They ate in silence. Since she had a head start on him, she finished first. The waitress refilled their cups and Evie drank from hers while she watched Clint finish eating.

"So why are you going to Helena?" she asked.

He didn't answer.

"It must have something to do with Granville Stewart."

"Why do you say that?"

"You asked me to point him out."

"Maybe I was just curious, too."

"Would you like me to tell you about Granville Stewart?"

"Sure."

"He's an ass."

"I got that much from you before."

"No, I said I didn't like him," she said. "That didn't make him an ass. But he is. It's his money."

"That makes him an ass?"

She nodded.

"I've met a lot of men like that."

"He's a good man, though," she said. "And good at what he does. He's just not very likable."

"Thanks," I said. "I'll keep that in mind when I meet him."

"Want to meet him now?"

"No," he said. "On the stage is soon enough."

"Okay," she said. "That might be interesting to watch."

SIX

As it turned out, they didn't meet on the stage. Granville Stewart didn't seem inclined to introduce himself to the other passengers. But he did watch, and listen, while they introduced themselves to each other.

The couple turned out to be Mr. and Mrs. Brownsville. They were traveling to Helena from the East, where Mr. Brownsville was going to administer to a flock as a preacher.

"Are you ordained?" Evie asked him.

"Oh, no," Mr. Brownsville said, "but it's a calling. You can't ignore a calling, you know."

"No," Evie said, "I guess not."

"You're a newspaperwoman," Brownsville said. "That must have been a calling to you."

"Maybe," Evie said. "I guess I never thought about it that way."

"And you, sir?" Brownsville asked. "What is your name?"

"Clint Adams."

There was a flicker of recognition in the eyes of Granville Stewart, but he still chose not to join in the conversation.

"Clint Adams," the preacher said with a frown. "That name does sound familiar."

"Maybe it's just that kind of name," Clint said.

Evie Loomis smiled behind her hand.

Stringer Jack looked up from the fire as Dutch Louie rode into camp. He had ridden into Judith Gap to see what the town was talking about. Apparently, he'd heard something that got him excited, because he was off the horse before it stopped running.

"What are you so excited about?" Jack asked.

"I thought you should know," Louie said, "Stewart is on the stage to Helena. Left this mornin'."

Stringer Jack rubbed his jaw. Perhaps it would be to their advantage to take the man out of the play early.

"It'll take 'em a day and a half, at least." He looked at Brocky Gallagher, who was hunkered down next to him. "Take a few men."

"Kill him?"

Jack nodded.

"What about the other passengers?"

"Might as well kill 'em all," Jack said. "Make it look like a robbery. With Granville Stewart gone, the Bitterroot Valley is ours for the taking."

"Who do I take?" Gallagher asked.

"Anybody," Jack said. "Take four men."

Gallagher stood up, walked over to a group of men, and pointed out four of them.

"Saddle up!" he said.

"Make it quick and easy, Brocky," Jack said. "No mistakes."

"No mistakes, boss," Gallagher said. "Got it."

They stopped at a stagecoach station to rest the horses and get a meal into the driver and passengers, but then continued on through the night in hopes of arriving in Helena before dark the next day.

Granville Stewart had only agreed to take the stage after a meeting with the agent, who assured him the coach would drive through the night and get him there the next day.

They all dozed through the night. Clint opened his eyes at first light while the others still slept. Then he noticed that Stewart was also awake.

The man looked at him, then smiled and said, "What's takin' the Gunsmith to Helena?"

Clint shrugged. "Haven't been there in a while," he said. "Thought I'd take a look while I was in Montana."

"And then head back to Judith Gap?"

"The sheriff's a friend of mine," Clint said. "Thought I'd spend a few days."

That seemed to satisfy Stewart, and he fell silent again.

The others woke then, and tried stretching.

"Do you think the driver might stop so we could stretch properly?" the preacher asked.

"No more stops," Stewart said. "We have a schedule to keep." This was the first time he'd spoken to anyone other than Clint.

The preacher blinked at Stewart and said, "I was just wondering—"

"No more stops," he said firmly.

"Well!" the preacher's wife said, but Stewart ignored her.

SEVEN

Brocky Gallagher reined in his horse and stared down the hill at the stagecoach traveling the road to Helena.

"We gonna take 'em now, Brocky?" one of the men asked.

"Let's ride on ahead and cut 'em off," Brocky said. "We'll take 'em then."

"How many passengers are there?" another man asked.

"Don't know," Brocky said, "but we know Stewart's there."

"What do we do with the others?"

Gallagher looked at the four men riding with him and said, "We kill 'em."

"All of 'em?" somebody asked.

"All of 'em."

"Any women?" another asked.

Gallagher grinned and said, "I guess we're gonna find out."

"I hope there's some good-lookin' women," one of the men said.

"What's the difference?" another said. "Free poon is free poon."

"Whoa!"

Clint heard the driver yell as he reined his team in.

"We're stopping," the preacher said. "I wonder why."

The preacher's wife gave Granville Stewart a hard look as if to say, "There, we are stopping!"

"Everybody out!"

"It's a robbery," Evie said, sounding excited.

"We don't have anything on this stage to steal," Stewart said. "That's not right."

"You have a gun?" Clint asked him.

"Yes." Stewart touched the space beneath his left arm, the weapon hidden by his jacket.

"You move when I do, okay?" Clint said.

"Right."

"Wait," the preacher said. "There's no need to kill—"

"Shut up, Preacher," Stewart said. "You're completely out of your element here."

"When the shooting starts," Clint told the others, "hit the deck."

"What? What? What's he mean?" the preacher's wife asked.

"The ground," Evie said. "He wants us to drop to the ground."

"But . . . my dress . . ."

"It's either get your dress dirty," Evie said, "or get killed."

"Oh, dear!"

"Come on, come on!" a man shouted. "Everybody out!"

Clint opened the door and stepped out. He saw five men, all mounted, holding guns. Their faces were not covered, so it was obvious this was not a robbery. They were here to kill. His guess was they were after Stewart, but when they killed him, they'd have to kill everyone.

Stewart stepped out, then the preacher. After that, Clint and Stewart helped the ladies out.

"Collect their valuables," one man ordered, obviously the leader.

The stage driver was still up top, but he'd dropped the reins and his hands were up. Clint didn't know if he'd be able to rely on the man when the shooting started.

One man got off his horse, took off his hat, and came up to the passengers.

"Wallets, jewelry," he said. "Come on!"

"Take their guns first!" the leader called.

As if he hadn't heard, the man passed his hat in front of each person, then stopped when he came to Evie.

"I'm gonna have a good time with you," he said, smiling, licking his lips lasciviously.

"How are you gonna do that without a dick?" she asked sweetly.

"What—" Before he could get another word out, she kicked him in the crotch. His eyes popped and he staggered back, grabbing for his gun.

Clint drew quickly and shot the man in the chest even before the full magnitude of the pain in his crotch could register.

He turned his gun on the mounted men, firing quickly. Behind him he was aware of Stewart's gun being fired.

The mounted killers were completely surprised, except for the leader. Angry that his man had ignored him, he wheeled his horse and got out of there while his men were being gunned down.

They all dropped from their saddles to the ground, dead.

"One is getting away!" Evie called.

"Let him," Stewart said. "He can tell his bosses that he failed."

Clint reloaded his gun before returning it to his holster, then checked on all the fallen men.

"They're all dead," he said.

"I'll say a prayer—" the preacher started, but Stewart stopped them.

"They don't deserve prayers, Preacher," the rancher said. "They were gonna kill all of us."

"You don't know that," the preacher's wife said.

"Yes," Stewart said, "I do. They were trying to kill me, and then they'd have to kill the rest of you."

"Their faces weren't covered," Clint pointed out, "so he's right. They were going to kill all of us."

"Oh dear," she said, looking at her husband. "What kind of a world have we come to?"

"This is the West, lady," Stewart said. "You better get used to it."

They collected their belongings and then started to get back into the stage.

"Aren't you going to bury them?" the preacher asked.

"Not a chance," Stewart said.

When the others were boarded, Clint and Stewart walked to the bodies.

"You know any of them?" Clint asked.

"No, never saw them."

"What about the one that got away?"

"No, not him either. All strangers, but they were guns for hire, so they would be strangers, wouldn't they?"

"I suppose so. You did okay back there."

"Why wouldn't I?" Stewart asked. "I've been fighting for what I want and have for years." He walked back to the stage. "Let's get moving!" he shouted to the driver.

The man saluted.

Clint walked back to the stage, waited for Granville Stewart to get in, and then climbed in behind him.

EIGHT

The attempted murder of all the passengers had not delayed them for very long, so the stage pulled into Helena while it was still light.

"Take my luggage to the Cattleman's Club," Stewart shouted up to the driver.

"Yes, sir."

He turned and walked away from the stagecoach without a word to any of the other passengers.

The stage had stopped directly in front of a hotel, so Clint grabbed his saddlebags, bade good-bye to the preacher and his wife, and Evie Loomis, and went inside to check in.

Evie came in right behind him and said, "I'll be staying here, too."

"Then by all means," he said, "you check in first."

"Why, thank you, sir."

She stepped up to the front desk and registered while Clint stood directly behind her, smelling her hair.

Behind him he heard the couple enter, the preacher and his wife, and they were arguing.

"I want to go back home, James," she said.

The preacher, James Brownsville, said, "Now now, Mother, we can't let a little trouble send us running back, can we? Besides, there's nothing left back there for us."

"My family is there," she argued.

"As I said," he reiterated, "nothing back there for us."

Evie finished registering and turned quickly, running into Clint's chest.

"Oh, sorry. I'm on the second floor. See you later?"

"Sure."

She went up as Clint stepped forward and registered. There were three stories to the hotel, and he was also placed on the second floor. He hoped the Brownsvilles would be put on the third. He didn't want to hear any more of the woman's whining.

That was probably unfair, he thought, as he went up the stairs. The woman didn't seem well suited for a life in the West.

He left his saddlebags and rifle in his room, then left to go in search of a cold beer.

Helena was many times the size of Judith Gap, but the bustling seemed to be along the same lines. He walked past a proper police station, but Piven had mentioned a sheriff still in town. He decided not to stop in and talk to the police. He'd wait until he found Sheriff Dan Lewis's office.

He came to the King's Ransom Saloon before finding

the sheriff's office, and so felt a responsibility to stop in and have at least one cold beer.

In keeping with its name, it was a grand place, with gaming tables strewn about and a stage up at the front. It was a saloon and music hall apparently.

It was busy at early evening, and bound to get busier as the covers came off the gaming tables, and the saloon girls came out to serve the customers. He wondered if there would be any music that night.

He elbowed himself a space at the bar and ordered a beer from one of the three bartenders.

"Nice and cold, friend," the barman said, setting it in front of Clint.

"Thanks."

"Fresh off the stage?"

"How can you tell?"

"I have a knack for faces," the bartender said. "Haven't seen yours before."

Clint studied the man. Of the three barmen, he was the middle one, in his forties. The oldest was in his fifties, moving very deliberately, and the youngest was in his thirties, moving about with great energy.

"What brings you to town?" the barman asked.

"Just having a look," Clint said. "I was here once, long ago."

"Has it changed?"

"Very much."

"Well, if you have any questions, flag me down," the barman said, and was off to serve others.

Clint nursed his beer while the tables got busy. Suddenly, there was room at the bar as men approached their games of choice—blackjack, roulette, poker, faro. The King's Ransom had it all.

When he'd finished with his beer, he waved at the barman to come over.

"'Nother one?"

"Maybe later," Clint said. "Can you tell me where to find the sheriff's office?"

"We have a real police station now, if you've got a legal problem."

"No," Clint said, "I just need to see Sheriff Lewis."

"Swell," the man said, "better get to him soon. His deputy just left here with a bottle."

"Just direct me," Clint said.

NINE

Clint followed the bartender's directions and found the sheriff's office. Compared to the fairly new appearance of the police station, this was a hole. He opened the door and entered. There were two men inside, having a conversation.

"Why can't I have a drink, Sheriff?" one man asked. He was younger, wearing a deputy's badge.

"Because whiskey's not good for you," the other man said. He was older, close to sixty, wearing the sheriff's badge.

"But you drink it."

"It's a bad habit I'm too old to break," the sheriff said.

"But Dan—"

"Go and do your rounds, Andy," the sheriff said.

"Yes, sir."

The deputy put his hat on and headed for the door, That was when both men saw Clint.

"Keep goin', Andy," the sheriff said. "I'll take care of this gentleman."

"Yes, sir."

The deputy went past Clint and out the door.

The sheriff took the time to uncork the bottle and poured himself a drink. Two fingers, Clint noticed.

"Can I help you, sir?" he asked, sitting back with his glass.

"Most sheriffs drink their whiskey from a coffee mug," Clint said.

"Well, I like glass," Dan Lewis said. "I keep one in the office just for whiskey."

Clint nodded.

"Still wanna talk to me?" the lawman asked.

"Yes," Clint said. "I bring greetings from Nat Piven."

"Ah," Lewis said, "you're Clint Adams."

"That's right."

"I got Piven's telegram," Lewis said. "Have a seat."

"Thanks."

"Drink?"

"I prefer beer."

"How about coffee?" Lewis asked. "I have mugs for that."

"Sure."

"Help yourself."

Clint looked around, saw possibly the oldest potbellied stove he'd encountered in a while. There was a small table next to it with mugs on it. He walked over and poured himself a coffee, brought it back to his chair.

"What can I do for you?" Lewis asked.

"Piven didn't tell you?"

"You tell me."

"I want to get into the Cattleman's Club."

"What for?"

"There's a meeting of cattlemen there."

"And you wanna attend?"

"No."

"Then what?"

"I want to eavesdrop."

"Ah. On whose behalf?"

"Sheriff Piven."

"Why?"

"Because he's charged with keeping the law along the Musselshell, and I want to help him."

"Why?"

"He's my friend."

"Are you a deputy?"

"No."

"Why not?"

"I don't wear a badge anymore," Clint said, "if I can help it."

"But you did once."

"A long, long time ago."

"What makes you think I can get you into the Cattleman's Club?"

"Piven said you could."

"We have a modern police department here now, you know," he said, sipping his whiskey.

"I saw."

"What do you think of modern police departments?"

"I don't have a sweeping opinion," Clint said.

Lewis grinned, showing one missing tooth in a mouth of otherwise well-cared-for white ones.

" 'Sweeping opinion,' " he said, chuckling.

"I judge them individually," Clint went on, "and I don't know anything about Helena's police department."

Lewis sat forward, poured himself another drink.

"That why you drink?" Clint asked. "Because of the police department?"

Lewis sat back again.

"I drink because I'm too old to break bad habits."

"Got any other bad habits?"

"Yes," Sheriff Dan Lewis said.

"What?"

"Doin' favors for friends."

"Like Nat Piven?"

Lewis nodded.

"So you'll get me into the Cattleman's Club?"

"Yes," Lewis said, "I'll get you into the Cattleman's Club. Can I finish my drink first?"

"The drink, or the bottle?"

Lewis shrugged.

"Same thing."

"How about we do it in the morning?" Clint asked. "Before the drink?"

"Sure," Lewis said. "Come by and get me when you're ready."

"Are they meeting tomorrow?"

"Yes," Lewis said, "but not early."

"Okay." Clint put the coffee mug on the desk. "Thanks for the coffee."

"You didn't drink it."

"It's terrible."

"Why do you think I drink whiskey?"

"See you tomorrow, Sheriff Lewis."

"Hold on a second," Lewis said.

"What?"

"I got a report from the stage line today that somebody tried to rob the stage you were on."

"Oh, that."

"Yeah, oh that. You shot some men."

"I shot some, yeah, but Granville Stewart shot the rest."

"I talked to him. He says he shot one, you shot the rest."

"Yeah, well, I was faster than him. Am I in trouble?" he asked.

"Naw, the stage driver says you both saved the stage from bein' robbed."

"Then what's the problem?"

"I don't know who's got jurisdiction, me, Piven, or somebody in between," Lewis said. "But don't worry, we'll work it out. Meanwhile, one of the men got away. You know him?"

"No," Clint said.

"Okay," Lewis said. "I'll see you tomorrow."

Lewis saluted Clint with his glass. Clint liked the old lawman.

TEN

Clint went back to the King's Ransom and had another beer. The bartender greeted him with a smile and Clint asked him to stay after he brought him his beer.

"What's on your mind?"

"Tell me about the Cattleman's Club."

"What about it?"

"What's it like?"

"Like a private saloon and hotel."

"So do any of the cattlemen ever drink here?"

"No," the bartender said. "They do their drinkin' in their club."

"So I wouldn't be running into any of them here tonight."

"No," the barman said. "They're too good to drink here, and this is the best place in town."

Clint looked at the stage. The curtains were closed.

"Any music tonight?"

"Nope. We don't have anyone booked in to entertain for a while."

"Do they have entertainment at the Cattleman's Club?" Clint asked.

"Depends on what you consider entertainment."

Someone called for a drink. The bartender yelled to one of the other bartenders to handle it.

"You the head bartender?" Clint asked.

"How'd you guess?"

"What's your name?"

"Eddie."

"Eddie," Clint said, "what kind of entertainment do they have at the Cattleman's Club?"

"The female kind."

"Ah."

"Why you so interested?"

"I'm going over there tomorrow."

"You think you're gonna get in?"

"I think so."

"If you do," Eddie said, "lemme know what it's like inside."

"Okay."

Clint put his empty mug down, started to leave.

"Hey."

"What?"

"What's your name?" Eddie asked.

"Clint Adams."

Eddie hesitated, then said, "Yeah, you'll get in."

ELEVEN

When Clint got to his hotel and entered, he found Evie Loomis in the lobby.

"Where are you coming from?" she asked.

"The saloon. What are you doing out and about after dark?" he asked.

"As a reporter, I can't very well be afraid of the dark," she said. "In fact, I had a late supper and was just getting back."

"Did you find somebody who would submit to your interviews?"

"As a matter of fact, I did," she said. "Two of the cattlemen who are going to be at the meeting tomorrow."

"Really? I'd be interested in what they had to say," he commented.

"Well, you'll have to wait until I write it up for the paper . . . unless . . ."

"Unless what?"

"Unless you want to buy me some coffee now and

answer some questions," she said. "Then I'll answer some of yours."

"I'll answer some questions," he said. "I won't submit to an interview."

"What's the difference?"

"I'll let you know as we go along. Shall we go right in here?"

The hotel dining room was still open so they went inside and got a table. The place was almost empty—only one other table occupied—so they didn't have to wait at all for their coffee.

"All right," she said. "What are you doing in Helena?"

"The same thing you are. I'm interested in the meeting tomorrow."

"But why? You don't live—"

"My turn," he said. "What two cattlemen did you talk to tonight?"

"Frank McAuliffe and Harry Jenkins."

"Local?"

"They're both about an hour out of town."

"Are their ranches on the Musselshell?"

"Near it," she said. "I'm sure they water their stock there."

"And what—"

"My turn!"

He sat back and smiled.

"Go ahead."

"Are you here to sell your gun to somebody?" she asked.

"I don't sell my gun, Miss Loomis," he said, "so the answer's no. My turn. What do you believe the cattlemen are going to be discussing tomorrow?"

She was still frowning at the answer to her last question.

"Well, one thing I thought they would be discussing was hiring you," she said, "but if you say that's not why you're here . . . maybe they'll be discussing hiring someone else."

"Seems you ought to check and see if you've got any hired guns in town."

"You mean other than you?"

"I am not a hired gun," he said carefully. "If you write anything about me in your newspaper, make sure you write that."

"I will," she said. "I'm sorry, it's just . . . your reputation . . ."

"As a reporter, you should know better than to blindly accept someone's reputation."

"So you're telling me nobody's reputation is to be believed?"

"Believe half of it," he said, "and expect the other half to be a lie."

"Can I quote you on that?"

"Yes," he said, "on that you can."

Clint allowed Evie a few more questions, but he was really done talking to her. After their coffee he walked out to the lobby with her.

"Are you off to the saloon for some gambling now?" she asked.

"Is that something else you heard about me?" he asked.

"I was just—"

"No," he said, cutting her off, "when I ran in to you, I

was heading back to my room. I'm going to turn in early. I'm sorry if that doesn't fit in with the picture you have of me in your head."

"Look, I'm sorry—"

"Maybe I'll see you tomorrow around the Cattleman's Club."

He left Evie Loomis standing dejected in the middle of the hotel lobby.

TWELVE

Stringer Jack looked up from the breakfast fire and saw Brocky Gallagher riding toward him. He would have had to ride all night to get back this soon.

He stood, holding a cup of coffee in his hand, and waited. The other spotted him and also stood. It escaped no one that he was returning alone.

Gallagher reined in and dismounted.

"I could use some coffee," he said, approaching the fire.

Stringer Jack hit him in the mouth. He landed on his back, gaping up at his boss.

"What was that for?"

"Where are the others?"

"They're . . . dead."

"And so are the passengers on the stage?" Jack asked. "Including Granville Stewart?"

"N-No."

"What happened?"

"Stewart had a gunhand on the stage with him," Gallagher said. "H-He took all of the others."

"But not you."

"N-No," Gallagher said. "I—I got away."

"You ran out on them?"

"Hey, this gun . . . he was fast. Fastest I ever saw, Jack."

"So," Jack said, "Stewart hired himself a gun. I wonder who it is."

Gallagher got to his feet.

"I don't know how many men could be that fast," he said.

"Get yourself some coffee," Jack said.

"What are we gonna do?" Silas Nickerson asked, coming up next to Jack.

"Nothin' changes," Jack said. "We're gonna go ahead as planned."

"But what's the plan?" Nickerson asked. "You ain't told us yet."

"I will," Jack said. "Soon."

"How soon?"

"Soon enough," Jack said. "I'm gonna get some more coffee."

Jack bent over the fire. His plan was his, and he'd share it with the rest of them soon enough.

Granville Stewart woke up the next morning in his room in the Cattleman's Club. He looked at the woman in bed next to him. She was of little consequence to him, other than the pleasure she'd given him during the night. Now she was an annoyance, a whore in his bed.

"Hey," he said, slapping her bare ass. "Wake up!"

"Wha—" she said, coming awake abruptly. "Jesus, mister, you kept me awake most of the night. Can't a girl get some sleep?"

"Yes, you can," he said, "but somewhere else."

"What?"

"Get dressed and get out!"

She rolled over. She had small breasts with brown nipples, skin that had looked pale the night before, but now looked pitted. In his haste to have a woman, he'd chosen badly, as far as looks went. In actuality, she was a talented whore, but in the morning sun . . .

"Come on, up and out," he said. "You've been paid already, so go!"

"Yeah, yeah, okay," she said, getting to her feet. Her butt was flat, her legs long and thin. He turned his head while she dressed. He'd take his time and choose better next time. Also, the Club had to raise its standards as far as the whores they brought in for their members.

"See ya next time," she said, and left the room.

No next time for you, he thought, and rolled over.

Clint woke with the sun streaming through his window. He rubbed his face and stared at the ceiling. He took a moment to bring it all into focus. He'd arrived in Judith Gap and, before he knew it, was on his way to Helena. Now he was supposed to get into the Cattleman's Club and . . . what?

He sat up, swung his feet to the floor, and realized how hungry he was. First things first. He got dressed and left the room to go downstairs and have breakfast.

* * *

As he entered the dining room, he saw the Brownsvilles seated at a table. He had no desire to sit and eat with them, so he simply exchanged nods with them and went to his own table. He hoped that Evie Loomis would not come in. He didn't want to eat with her either.

As it turned out, his only companion for breakfast would be Sheriff Dan Lewis, who walked in at that moment, spotted him, and headed over.

THIRTEEN

"Mind if I join you?" Lewis asked.

"Have a seat."

Lewis sat down.

"Breakfast?" Clint asked. "It's on me this time."

"Sure, why not?" Lewis said. "After that you wanna walk over to the Cattleman's Club?"

"You got any idea what time they're going to start their meeting?"

"I'm not sure," he said, "but what's the difference? Once you're in, you're in."

"Good point."

A waiter came over and they both ordered steak and eggs, Clint because that's what he ate when he wasn't on the trail, and the sheriff because it was the most expensive breakfast on the menu.

The waiter poured them some coffee and the sheriff drank.

"Better than your office coffee, huh?" Clint asked.

"No contest," Lewis said.

"How long have you been sheriff of Helena?" Clint asked.

"Too long, probably," Lewis said. "And long enough to know that loyalty means nothin'."

Clint could see that the man had been turned bitter by his years behind the badge. He wondered if the same would have happened to him if he'd pursued a career as a lawman.

"The new police department, you mean?"

"Yes," Lewis said. "The town fathers told me I could keep my badge, but that the laws would be enforced by the police."

"You have no authority at all?"

"No, I still do," Lewis said, "but I have to take a backseat to the new police chief."

"Why didn't they just make you the police chief?"

"That'd be a laugh," the sheriff said. "I wasn't about to wear that uniform. I woulda turned the job down, but they never offered it to me. They brought in a younger man from back East to set up the department, and hire all the men."

"What about your deputy?" Clint asked.

"Dumb as a stump," Lewis said. "But loyal."

"What about going somewhere else?"

"And doing what?" Lewis asked. "Who's gonna hire somebody my age to be a sheriff? Best I'd do is getting hired by some whippersnapper to be his deputy. That ain't for me."

"So you'll stay here as long as you can?"

"Why not?" he asked. "I get paid, I eat for free—as

long as it ain't somethin' like steak and eggs—I got a place to sleep . . ."

The lawman stopped talking as the waiter appeared with their plates. He poured them some more coffee and moved on.

Lewis started eating. Clint decided to eat in silence as long as the man wanted to.

"So why is the Gunsmith working with the sheriff of a place like Judith Pass?" he said finally.

"Nat's an old friend of mine. He sent me a telegram saying he needed me," Clint explained. "There's no money for a deputy, so he asked if I could help out."

"You get that a lot?" Lewis asked. "Being asked for help, I mean."

"Sometimes."

"You always respond?"

"Usually," Clint said. "It's how I get into most of my trouble."

"I would think carryin' around a reputation would get you into enough trouble."

"Oh yeah, that, too."

Lewis cut off a large hunk of steak and stuffed it into his mouth.

"This is great," he said. "Worth you comin' to town for me to get this. So how much trouble are you gonna cause?"

"I don't know," Clint said. "Are you worried?"

"Me? No, if you cause trouble, it'll be the police department's job to do somethin' about it, not me."

"Maybe I should stop in there, then," Clint said. "Let them know I'm in town."

"Sure, why not?"

"What's the chief's name?"

"Hm, uh, Paul . . . something. Pierce, that's it. Chief Pierce."

"What's he like?"

"Young, not forty yet," Lewis said. "I think he used to be a schoolteacher."

"Really?"

"Yeah, really," Lewis said, "but apparently he's studied some new policing techniques."

"Jesus," Clint said. "Would you like some more steak, Sheriff?"

"I sure would . . ."

FOURTEEN

Granville Stewart came down to the Cattleman's Club dining room and sat alone while he ate. Across the room four others were seated together, deep in conversation. They paused only when he entered, watched him walk to his table, and then went back to chattering like hens.

Before long Edward Quarterman walked in. Stewart had not seen the man in several months, but he looked as if he had aged years. This was the only man in the Club who he had any respect for.

"Edward!" he called, and waved.

The old man saw him, waved back, and crossed the room with a slow, almost painful gait.

"Join me for breakfast," Stewart said.

"It's very good to see you, Granville," Quarterman said, seating himself across the table from Stewart. "It's been a while."

"Yes," Stewart said. "It has. Let's order for you, and then we'll talk."

"I need something . . . soft," Quarterman said.

"Of course."

Stewart called the waiter over and ordered some oatmeal for his old friend.

"And some tea," Quarterman said.

"Yes, sir," the waiter said.

They waited until Quarterman had both his tea and his breakfast in front of him before they started to talk.

"Look at them," Stewart said. "Talking like a bunch of old women with their heads pressed together."

Quarterman looked over at them.

"Yes," he said, "they have a lot of problems. They need a solution."

"And what am I?" Stewart asked. "A problem or a solution?"

"I think they believe you are one of each, Gran," Quarterman said.

"And what do you think, Edward?"

"I think you should let bygones be bygones and work with them," Quarterman said.

"Bygones?" Stewart asked. "After what they did? Voting me out as president?"

"That was several years ago, Gran," Quarterman said. "You've forgiven me, haven't you?"

"Just barely."

"Well," Quarterman said, "if you're not here to forgive them, what are you here for?"

Stewart smiled, chewed some eggs, swallowed, and said, "I'm here to make them all eat dirt."

* * *

After breakfast Sheriff Lewis was ready to walk Clint over to the Cattleman's Club.

"I think," Clint said as they stepped outside, "I'll go over to the police department first."

"You ever been in one of them modern police station?" Lewis asked.

"Yes."

"Lots of men runnin' around in silly uniforms," the old sheriff said. "I mean, at least if they'd wear blue like the Army, they wouldn't look so stupid."

"What color do they wear?"

"Gray," Lewis said. "Ain't that a hoot? Like nobody remembers the war?"

"You think people will hold the color of their uniforms against them?"

"Why not?" Lewis asked. "It's been done before."

"Where can I meet you?" Clint asked.

"Just come to my office when you're ready," Lewis said. "I'll take you over there."

"Okay," Clint said.

Lewis slapped Clint on the back.

"Thanks for breakfast, and give the chief my regards, will ya?"

He turned and headed off toward his office.

Clint found the brand, spanking new police department building and entered. As Lewis had said, there were men inside wearing gray uniforms, looking kind of silly.

One of them came over to him. Young kid—twenties—looking very eager to please.

"Can we help you?"

"I'd like to see the chief."

"Can't I help you with something?"

"I'd really just like to see the chief," Clint said. "Chief Pierce, right?"

"That's right," the young man said. "Can I tell him who wants to talk to him?"

"Yes," Clint said. "Tell him my name is Adams, Clint Adams."

"All right," the policeman said, "Clint . . . wait, Adams?"

"Yes."

Suddenly nervous, the man asked, "The, uh, Gunsmith?"

"That's right."

"I'll tell him," he said. "I'll just go and, uh . . ."

He hurried off.

FIFTEEN

When Chief Paul Pierce came out to meet Clint, he saw what the sheriff had meant. Whether Pierce used to be a schoolteacher or not, he *looked* like one.

"Mr. Adams?" Pierce asked.

"That's right."

"A pleasure, sir," Pierce said, shaking his hand. "Will you come with me to my office?"

"Sure."

Clint followed the man to a back office, where he closed the door, giving them some privacy. It was a small office with only the necessities—two chairs, a desk with a chair, and one file cabinet.

"Can I offer you some coffee?" the chief asked, seating himself. "It's not very good, I'm afraid."

"I'll skip it, then. Thanks."

"So what brings you to my office today?"

"Actually, I got into town last night and just thought I'd stop in, pay my respects, and let you know I'm here."

"Well, I appreciate that," the chief said. "I always like to know when somebody with your reputation comes to Helena."

Clint could see why Sheriff Lewis was bitter. This man looked like a teacher, and hardly looked thirty, although he was certainly older than that. The four or five uniformed men outside the office all seemed to be thirty or less.

"Your department looks fairly, uh, young," he observed.

"Yes, I'm afraid that's my fault," Pierce said, "although if I had a man of your caliber in town, I would offer him a job, regardless of age."

Clint supposed that was meant as a compliment.

"How many men do you have?" Clint asked.

"Well, we have twelve, although there are only five at a time on duty. We've been set up here for about six months, so we're still getting the kinks out."

"I suppose you've got a good working relationship with the sheriff?"

"Ah, Sheriff Lewis," Pierce said, shaking his head. "I'm afraid he's not very happy with us in general, and with me in particular."

"Oh, why's that?"

"Have you met the man?"

"Briefly."

"He's rather bitter about our department being brought into Helena," he said. "He would rather hang on to the old way. I'm afraid we don't have much contact with each other."

"That's too bad," Clint said. "Seems to me a man his

age would have a lot of experience you and your men might benefit from."

"Well," Pierce said, fiddling with a piece of paper on his desk, "I'm sure you're right, but as I said, the man is bitter and quite unwilling to work with us."

"Too bad."

"Was there anything else?" Pierce asked. "I'm afraid I have quite a bit of work to do."

"No, that's it," Clint said. "Just wanted to check in and let you know I'm here."

"And not looking for trouble, right?"

Clint stood up and said, "Furthest thing from my mind."

Pierce stood and said, "Glad to hear it."

He extended his hand and Clint shook it.

"Banks!" the chief yelled.

The young officer who had spoken to him when he first entered came flying through the door.

"Yes, sir?"

"Please show Mr. Adams out."

"Yes, sir." Officer Banks stood aside. "Sir?"

Clint preceded the young man out of the office and they walked to the door together. He felt the eyes of the other men in the room follow him out.

Banks actually followed him out of the building and said, "Sir?"

"Yes?"

"I was just wondering if I could shake your hand, sir," Banks said. "I mean . . . you're a legend, sir."

"Am I?" Clint shook the young man's hand.

"Well, yes, sir. I've been hearing about you since I was a kid."

"Thanks."

"Sure wish we could have some time to talk. I'd love to hear about some of your experiences."

"Well, I wish I had time for that, too, Officer, but I'll be leaving town tomorrow. But I tell you what—I'll bet you could get a lot of interesting stories out of Sheriff Lewis."

"Him?"

"He's been a lawman for a long time," Clint said. "I'll bet he'd be real interesting—and helpful—to talk to."

"Well, I suppose . . ."

"You should stop in on him one evening," Clint said. "I'm sure he'd be happy to talk. Do you know him?"

"I've seen him around, sir," Banks said. "And I do know his deputy."

"There you go," Clint said. "Have the deputy introduce you."

"I might do that, sir," Banks said. "Thank you."

"Good."

Clint stepped down from the boardwalk and crossed the street. When he turned, the young officer was going back into the building. Clint headed for the sheriff's office.

SIXTEEN

The Musselshell was not a deep river. In fact, in many parts it was barely three feet deep, about a hundred yards wide. Easy to ride across, easy to drive stolen cattle back across.

Stringer Jack followed his men across the river. They were on their way to make what he called "a collection." Collect some cattle that didn't belong to them—yet.

He wasn't ready to hit the DHS spread, even in Granville Stewart's absence. They were, however, going to hit a neighboring spread and the word would certainly get back to the DHS.

Paddy Rose came riding up next to him.

"What?" he said.

"Nothin'," Rose said. "I just thought I'd ride along with ya, Jack."

"Ride on ahead, Paddy," he said. "I don't need company."

"Okay, Jack," Rose said. "Whatever you say."

Stringer Jack didn't have any desire to make friends with his men. Better they feared him than got friendly with him, or even respected him. He found fear to be the biggest tool in his arsenal.

It was a tool he was soon going to use on Granville Stewart.

Clint entered the sheriff's office, found the man sitting behind his desk with his feet up.

"Well, how did it go at the police department?" Lewis asked. "Find the chief a charming man?"

"No," Clint said. "I found him cold, and not very smart."

"There ya go."

"I told him he should take advantage of your experience."

Lewis laughed out loud at that.

"How did he take that?"

"Didn't take it very well," Clint said. "Told me how unfriendly you are."

"He's right, I am unfriendly," Lewis said. "I'm an unfriendly cuss." He dropped his feet to the floor. "You ready to go over to the Cattleman's Club?"

"I'm ready."

"Let's go."

He stood up, grabbed his hat, and led the way toward the door.

On the street Lewis asked, "You want me to get you through the door, or go in with ya and introduce you?"

"Introduce me to who?"

"There's a few ranchers who are old-timers," the sheriff

said. "That's how I get in. I'll introduce you to them, and then maybe they'll get you near that meetin'."

"Okay," Clint said.

"Or I could just slide you through the door and leave you on your own."

"I think I like the other way better," Clint said. "I could use an introduction."

"Yeah, okay," Lewis said, "but I gotta warn you, they're old cusses like me and not real likable. In fact, I'm more likable than any of them."

"Then I guess I'm really in trouble."

Lewis grinned at him and said, "Hey, that's what I'm tellin' ya."

They reached the Cattleman's Club, mounted the front steps. There was a man standing at the door.

"Stop here, please," he said, holding his hand out. He had a .45 on his hip.

"Harry, we go through this every time I come here," Lewis said.

"Sorry, Sheriff, but you gotta be somebody's guest. You know that."

"Talk to Considine or Old Man Fredericks," Lewis said. "Same as always."

"Wait here."

The man went inside.

"He does this every time," Lewis complained.

"He's got to justify his job, right?"

"Ahhh, everybody's gotta justify their jobs," the lawman said. "If I only had the money, I'd retire, get myself a little farm, or ranch. But not here. Not around here."

"Where?"

"New Mexico somewhere," Lewis said.

"I know somebody who has a ranch out there," Clint said. "His name's John—"

"Okay," Harry said, cutting Clint off. "You can go in. Who's this guy?"

"He's my guest," Lewis said. "Clint Adams."

"The Gunsmith?"

"That's right," the lawman said. "You wanna stop him from goin' in?"

Harry snorted.

"I don't get paid enough for that," he said. "Go ahead."

Clint and Sheriff Lewis entered the Cattleman's Club.

SEVENTEEN

As they entered, Clint could see where somebody had gone overboard trying to make the Cattleman's Club in Helena, Montana, look like the inside of a gambling palace in Portsmouth Square, San Francisco. It didn't work. What they ended up with was a tacky-looking club interior that nobody in town knew the truth about.

"Tacky, ain't it?" the sheriff asked, surprising him.

"Somebody had a dream and tried to make it come true," Clint said.

"Yep," Lewis said. "Looks like a whorehouse, don't it?"

"Oh, yeah."

"And a lot of these cattlemen treat it like a whorehouse, too."

"Girls for the members?"

"Yeah, any kind, any size," Lewis said.

"So it's just a big clubhouse."

"You got it."

"Okay," Clint said. "Introduce me to your friends, and then I guess you can go."

"Maybe I'll hang around," Lewis said. "Always makes them uncomfortable when I'm here."

"Why?"

"Because I know they're all bungholes."

Lewis grabbed Clint's arm, steered him toward a man with white hair and a white beard.

"Daniel," the man said. "How nice. And you've brought a friend."

"This is Clint Adams," Lewis said. "This is George Fredericks, one of the biggest cattlemen in the state."

Clint shook the old man's hand, was careful with it because he was frail. He had a walking stick in his left hand.

"Mr. Adams, welcome to our club. Whataya think?"

"Well—"

"Never mind," he said. "It's horrible. Looks like a whorehouse."

"Yes, sir."

"What brings you to Helena?" Fredericks asked. "Looking for work?"

"No, sir."

"Too bad, I could use a man like you. We all could."

"Why is that?"

"Rustlers."

"You have the law to take care of them."

"Nat Piven's a good man, but he can't police the Musselshell alone."

"What about your new police department?"

"They are a city police department," Fredericks said.

"They don't take responsibility for anything that happens outside the city limits."

"And what about Sheriff Lewis here?"

"Dan's a throwback," the old man said. "He'd take a posse out in a minute to track these rustlers down."

"But?"

"But nobody will volunteer, and let's face it, he's too old for the saddle. Like me."

"I'm younger than you, you old coot," Lewis said.

"Still too old for the saddle, old friend," Fredericks said. "Take your friend around, Dan. Show him the whole place." Fredericks patted Clint on the arm. "Make everyone uncomfortable, Mr. Adams. They're all gonna wonder who you've come here to work for."

"I'll do my best," Clint said. "Pleasure to meet you, sir."

"You, too."

The old man hobbled away, leaning on his stick.

"Oldest member of the Club," Lewis said.

"Anyone else as old?"

"Almost," Lewis said. "I'll introduce you to Edward Quarterman. Almost as old as Fredericks, but richer."

"What's his background?"

"Same. Self-made, several of the other ranchers grew up working for him, went on to have their own places. Best known of those is Granville Stewart."

"I came in on the stage with him."

"He's a loner, even though he's a member of the Club. He probably came to town to see Quarterman, and to gloat over the others."

"Gloat?"

"They can't stop the rustlers. Granville Stewart doesn't think anyone can stop him."

"So if they all work together—"

"But they won't. These people can't work together. If they're not stabbing each other in the back, they're shootin' themselves in the foot."

"Like lots of towns."

"It's my feelin' the rustlers know this, and are gonna take advantage of it."

"You got any idea who's leadin' the rustlers?"

"I got a few ideas."

"Want to share?"

"Maybe later," Lewis said. "Let's make some more people uncomfortable. It's fun."

EIGHTEEN

Lewis introduced Clint to a few more cattlemen in passing, then entered the dining room.

"That's Quarterman," Lewis said, "sitting in the corner with—"

"Granville Stewart."

"Right. Wanna interrupt their breakfast?"

"Why not?"

They walked across the room. Stewart saw them, leaned forward, and said something to Quarterman. The older man turned his head as Clint and the sheriff reached him.

"Hello, Sheriff Lewis," Quarterman said. "And Mr. Adams. A pleasure to meet you."

"Clint Adams," the sheriff said, "meet Edward Quarterman. One of the biggest ranchers in the state."

"Third biggest," Quarterman said, then looked at Stewart and said, "Right?"

"I suppose."

"That would make you first," Clint said, looking at Stewart. "So who's second?"

"You met him," Lewis said. "That would be Fredericks."

"Doddering old man," Stewart said.

Quarterman looked at Stewart.

"He's two years younger than I am."

"Still doddering," Stewart said. "You, on the other hand, are not."

Clint noticed from their plates that they had finished their breakfasts some time ago.

"So when's the big meeting?" he asked.

Quarterman said, "About fifteen minutes. We've just been sitting here catching up."

"I hope you weren't planning on attending," Stewart said to Clint.

"Why would I?" Clint asked. "I'm not a cattleman, am I."

"But maybe you're here to work for one," Quarterman said. "Who would that be?"

"I don't know," Clint said, "since I'm not."

"So you say."

Quarterman removed his napkin from his neck and dropped it onto his plate. He then got to his feet slowly. Clint couldn't help thinking that a walking stick would have helped the man quite a bit.

"I'll see you in there, Granville."

"Right."

"Excuse me, gentlemen."

Clint and Lewis stepped aside to let the old gent go.

"What the hell are you doing, Sheriff?" Stewart demanded.

"Whataya mean?"

"Why did you bring Adams into the Club?"

"Why not? He wanted to see the inside. He didn't believe me when I told him it looked like a cheap whorehouse."

"But he was right." Clint sniffed. "It even smells like a cheap whorehouse."

Stewart stood up.

"Everybody knows that," he said to them. "It's no big secret."

"Then why doesn't anybody do anything about it?" Clint asked.

"Because we all like it this way," Stewart said. "Now if you'll excuse me."

He pushed past them, not bothering to wait until they stepped aside.

"He's a charmer," Clint said.

"Come on," Lewis said. "I'll show you where their little meeting is gonna happen."

Lewis walked Clint through the Club to a large room with many overstuffed red chairs. The wallpaper was red and gold.

"Jesus," Clint said. "Looks like the sitting room of a whorehouse."

"Exactly," Lewis said. "Actually, I kinda like this room. I sat with lots of whores in rooms like this over the years. Didn't you?"

"Early in my life," Clint said. "But after I got old enough, I stopped using them."

"Yeah, well," Lewis said, "I guess you didn't need to, huh?"

Clint turned and looked around. The doorway to the room was open, so there was no way to close it off. All Clint had to do was sit just outside the room to hear what was going on. That was all he'd told Nat Piven he would do. Listen.

"Okay," Clint said, "I think I've got what I wanted, Sheriff."

"Okay," Lewis said. "I gotta go do rounds and pretend I'm still a real sheriff anyway. Good luck. You can stay in here all day if you want."

NINETEEN

Clint picked his chair out, claimed it, and just waited.

A man named Ben Considine seemed to be officiating at the meeting. Clint had not been introduced to him.

The room began to fill up. Fredericks and Quarterman entered and sat in front. They were followed by several other men, and then Granville Stewart showed up.

"What the hell are you doin'?" he demanded of Clint.

"Me? I'm just sitting."

"You don't belong here."

"Really? I was told I could stay as long as I wanted to."

"Who told you that?"

"Granville?" someone said from the other room. "We're ready to start."

Stewart seemed unsure about what to do. Finally he pointed his finger at Clint.

"Just stay out of the way."

Clint spread his hands and said, "I wouldn't dream of interfering."

"See that you don't."

Stewart entered the room and took a seat.

Just before the meeting started, Clint noticed a disturbance near the front door. Harry, the doorman, was wrestling with someone who was hopelessly outmatched.

Evie Loomis.

How had she gotten into the Club?

"Let me go, you bully!" she shouted.

"Out you go, missy," Harry said. "You don't belong in here."

Clint left his seat.

"Let her go, Harry."

The big man looked at Clint, then dropped Evie like she was hot.

"B-But she don't belong in here," he stammered.

"Why don't we just say she's my guest?" Clint asked.

"Well . . . okay, Mr. Adams," the doorman said. "If you say so."

"I do."

"Fine."

The big man went back outside.

"Wow, thanks," Evie said, straightening her suit. She bent over, picked up her pad and pencil.

"If you want to take some notes, come with me," he said.

He took her back to where he'd been sitting, sat back down in his chosen chair. There were others, since most of the cattlemen were seated in the other room.

"Take your pick," he said.

"Is that—" she started, but he cut her off.

"Just sit down, be quiet," he said, "and listen."

* * *

The meeting was a sham, a waste. There was nothing for Clint to interfere with. The cattlemen started to discuss the problem of the rustlers, and ended up arguing over who should run the meeting, who was the real head of the Club, who should be doing what.

Finally, Granville Stewart stood up and said, "I only came here today to remind myself what a bunch of morons you all are. I'll take my leave now."

"Granville!" Edward Quarterman called.

Stewart stopped just outside the doorway. He ignored Clint and Evie.

"What, Edward?"

"We were counting on you to pull this all together, Gran," Quarterman said.

"Speak for yourself," Considine said.

"Shut up, Considine," Fredericks said.

"Gran—" Quarterman started again.

"Edward, I think I'm gonna leave you all on your own," Stewart said, turning back to the room. "In fact, that's what I think we should all do, stay on our own, defend our own property. That's what I intend to do."

"Granville—"

Stewart turned and walked away.

"That's all he came here to do?" Clint said to Evie Loomis.

"Not surprising," she said. "He hates them all."

"Why would he even bother to come all this way just to tell them they're a bunch of morons?"

"He came all this way to lord it all over them," Evie said.

"And now he'll go back?"

"Probably."

"On the next stage?"

"I imagine," she said. "That's what I'm booked on, the next stage out." She stood up, closed her pad. "What about you? When are you going back to Judith Gap?"

"I don't know," Clint said. "I think I expected something more out of this little trip."

"Really?" she asked. "I got what I wanted, so I guess I'll see you back in Judith."

"Evie?"

"Yes."

"Is that next stage today?"

"Now, it's in the morning."

"So you'll be spending one more night in the hotel?" he asked.

"Yes."

"Then I'll see you at the hotel."

"Yes," she said, "you might very well."

She turned and left. On her heels the cattlemen began to leave the meeting room after what Clint could only describe as a complete farce.

The last two out were the two oldest, Fredericks and Quarterman.

"Mr. Adams," Quarterman said. "Would you accompany us to the dining room for a cup of coffee?"

"The both of you?"

"Yes," Fredericks said, "the both of us. But I'm afraid we'll all three have to walk at my speed, if that's all right."

"Yes," Clint said, "of course, at your speed."

TWENTY

They finally got seated in the dining room and a waiter brought them all coffee.

"I assume you heard all that," Quarterman said. "That poor excuse for a meeting?"

"Uh, yeah, I did hear it. I was kind of surprised. I mean, I've been to some other Cattlemen's Clubs—especially in Texas—and they seem to work a lot more closely together than you fellows do."

"Yes," Fredericks said. "I would bet they do."

"It doesn't sound like you're going to get much done about these rustlers. Unless you can manage to fight them off on your own."

"That's the way we used to do it in the old days," Fredericks said. "Remember, Edward?"

"Yes," Quarterman said, "on our own, or together, you and I."

"These others, with their more modern operations,

don't know the first thing about dealing with rustlers," Fredericks said.

"And they won't listen to their elders," Quarterman said.

"Or their betters."

"That's why we thought we'd talk to you," Quarterman said.

"Seein' as how you're here already."

"Talk to me . . . about what?"

"We want to hire you," Fredericks said.

"We'll pay you very well," Quarterman said.

"To do what?"

"What?" Fredericks said. "Why, track these rustlers down."

"And kill them."

"We'll pay you," Fredericks said, "by the head."

"You mean," Clint asked, "like a bounty."

"Yes, that's exactly what we mean," Fredericks said.

"A bounty," Quarterman said.

"Well, gentlemen," Clint said, pushing his chair back and getting to his feet, "it's been interesting."

"B-But . . ." Fredericks said.

"You haven't told us how much—" Quarterman said.

"I'm not for hire, gents," Clint said. "Not now, not ever. I don't work for bounty."

"But . . . you're the Gunsmith, right?" Fredericks asked.

"A man with a reputation," Quarterman said.

"You need to hire yourselves another man with a reputation," Clint said. "Find somebody else."

"Well . . . how are we supposed to do that?" Fredericks demanded, pounding his walking stick on the floor.

"You must've come here to work for somebody," Quarterman said. "Otherwise, what the hell are you doing here?"

"That," Clint said, "is my business. Good day, gents."

When he got outside, he found Sheriff Lewis standing there, whittling. The doorman, Harry, was trying to kick the shavings off the boardwalk and into the street.

"What are you doing here?" Clint asked.

"Finished my rounds and thought I'd come over and see how the meetin' went."

"How do you think it went?"

"Well, I saw Stewart leave pretty quick, so my guess is it was a mess."

"A helluva mess," Clint said.

"Surprise you?"

"Well, yeah."

"These fellas just can't work together," Lewis said, "except for the two old ones."

"They tried to hire me," Clint said. "They wanted to put a bounty on the heads of the rustlers."

"You could've made yourself a bundle that way," Lewis said.

"I suppose," Clint said, "but that's not the way I make money."

"So what now?" Lewis asked. "Back to Judith Gap?"

"I suppose."

"Next stage in the mornin', I hear," the sheriff said. "That should be an interestin' ride back to Judith Gap, you and Granville Stewart in the stage together."

"Oh, I don't think so."

"Why's that?"

"Well, he didn't talk much on the way here," Clint said. "I don't think he's going to talk that much on the way back. Besides, we'll have Evie Loomis on the stage, as well."

"The newspaper gal? She's a cute one."

"Yeah, and she's got lots of questions."

"Maybe she'll get him talking."

"I doubt it," Clint said. "She hates him."

"Well," Lewis said, "all I can say is, I'm sorry I'm not gonna be on that stage."

TWENTY-ONE

Clint agreed to meet the sheriff at the King Ransom's Saloon sometime after supper, and the two went their separate ways. Clint was finding the old lawman a lot more likable than he let on. Maybe it was the sheriff's cantankerous attitude that he liked. Or maybe he just sympathized with him.

He should have asked the lawman where he could get a good steak.

When Granville Stewart left the meeting, he went back to his room. He didn't want to run into any of the cattlemen, especially his old friend, Edward Quarterman, or the decrepit George Fredericks. He knew, in the old days, those two would have gotten on horses and tracked down the rustlers themselves. Well, that was what he intended to do, and it wasn't to help anyone but himself.

So far, the rustlers had not hit his DHS Ranch, but he expected that to change soon enough.

He felt like having a whore. He tugged on the pull cord that would bring a bellman running.

"Well," Edward Quarterman said to George Fredericks, "that didn't go well."

"What's the man getting on his high horse about?" Fredericks asked. "He's a damn gun for hire, isn't he?"

"Apparently not."

Fredericks banged his stick on the floor.

"If it wasn't for this damned leg, I'd get on a horse myself."

"And I'd be right with you, but let's face it, George. Those days are gone for us."

"And what about your protégé?" Fredericks asked.

"Granville has a mind of his own," Quarterman said. "But if he does decide to go after these rustlers himself, for his own reasons, then we benefit, don't we?"

"I suppose we do."

"And Adams is here for some reason," Quarterman went on. "It can't be a coincidence."

"So you think he's going after the rustlers after all?" Fredericks asked.

"One way or another," Quarterman said, "for one reason or another, yes."

"Well, then," Fredericks said, "let's have another drink."

Quarterman would have preferred to have a whore, but alas, those days were gone, as well.

Sheriff Dan Lewis went back to his office, sat at his desk with a drink in his hand and his feet up on his desk. He had the feeling that Clint Adams was going to make fools out of everyone when it came to catching these rustlers. He just wished it would extend to Chief Paul Pierce and his damned police department. The man was more politician than lawman, the way he was keeping himself out of this rustler business.

He just wished he could be a fly on the wall in Judith Gap.

Evie Loomis felt she had made progress with Clint Adams at the Cattleman's Club. Perhaps even made up for insulting him earlier in the day.

But maybe there was another method she could use to worm her way into his confidence.

TWENTY-TWO

When the knock came at Clint's door, he drew his gun from his holster, wondering how many times he'd done this. Countless hotels, countless knocks at the door, and what? Half the time opening the door was good news, and half it was bad.

What would it be this time?

When he opened the door, Evie Loomis smiled, held up a bottle and two glasses.

"I hate to drink alone," she said. Then she noticed the gun. "Well, I guess that shouldn't surprise me. You must always answer the door that way."

"Are you still trying to interview me?" he asked, holding the gun behind his back.

"That wasn't a question," she said. "It was just a comment." She wiggled the bottle. "But this is a question. How about it?"

"Sure," he said, "why not. Come on in."

He went back to the bedpost and holstered his gun.

When he turned, she had already poured whiskey into the two glasses.

"What are we drinking to?" he asked.

"Nothing in particular," she said, handing him a glass. "I felt like a drink, and like I said, I don't like to drink alone. It makes me sad."

"Why?"

She shrugged.

"Aren't people usually sad when they're drinking alone?"

"I don't know," he said. "I spend a lot of time drinking alone and I'm not sad."

"Well, I guess that makes you an exception to the rule, Mr. Adams." She raised her glass in a salute, and then poured some more. That was when he realized she had already done some drinking alone.

"You know," she said, "when I first came west, I thought I'd be working for a newspaper in Dodge City and Tombstone. Instead, I'm in Judith Gap. That's enough to make me drink alone, don't ya think?"

"I don't know," he said. "Even if you were in Dodge City or Tombstone, they're not the towns they once were. There's probably more going on in Judith Gap right now, with the rustlers and all."

"You know," she said, scrunching her face up, "you're right, Clint Adams. Right as rain." She drained her drink, poured herself another. He finished his first and held his glass out. If he helped her get to the bottom of the bottle, maybe that would stop her from drinking too much.

"There ya go," she said, topping off his drink. Then she shook the bottle. "It's almost empty. I musta drank more than I thought before I decided to share. I could go get another bottle—"

"No," he said, "that won't be necessary. We don't need another bottle."

"We don't?"

"No, we don't."

"Hmm," she said, "maybe you're right."

She drank down what was left in her glass, then upended the bottle and finished that. There was a little dripping down her chin, but she left it there. He drank the last of his and set the glass aside.

"You know what I always wondered?" she asked.

"What?"

"I always wondered if, after I've been drinking, my tongue tastes like whiskey. Now, I can't really tell because it's already in my mouth."

"Evie—"

"But maybe you can help me," she said, coming closer to him. She was still dressed in the suit she'd been wearing all day, but the jacket was unbuttoned and, somehow, some of the shirt buttons beneath were also undone. He saw the soft, pale swell of her breasts.

"Evie, you're drunk—"

"And you think you can take advantage of me?" she asked. "Well, Mr. Clint Adams, let me tell you something." She pounded him on the chest with her little fist, to make her point. "I came here to take advantage of you. Whataya think of that?"

"Well, I think it's very progressive of you."

"Progressive," she said. "Ha! Just help me out here. What does my tongue taste like?"

Before he could say or do anything else, she put her

hand behind his neck and pulled him down to her. When their lips met, she opened her mouth and pushed her tongue into his mouth. She gave him a good, long taste before drawing back.

"So?" she asked. "What's the verdict, Mr. Gunsmith?"

"I'm not sure, Miss Loomis," he said, putting his arms around her. "I think I need another long taste."

She was about to say something else but he cut her off by pulling her to him and kissing her again.

TWENTY-THREE

Clint decided that Evie might have been drunk, but she wasn't too drunk to know what she was doing. When he stripped off her clothes and got her naked, it was because she wanted to be naked.

He got on his knees in front of her, kissed her belly and her navel while massaging the cheeks of her ass. She moaned, put her hands on the top of his head, and pushed him farther down. She spread her legs so he could work on her with his tongue, and she started to grunt as his tongue moved up and down over her. She became very wet, and the room grew pungent with the smell of her.

"Oooh, God," she said, and suddenly backed up to the bed and fell onto it, on her back. He went with her, slid his hands beneath her butt, and continued to lick and suck her until she started to drum on his back with her heels. Her arms and legs flailed about uncontrollably as she bucked and writhed on the bed.

He gave her a moment to collect herself as he stood

up and took off his own clothes. She was still breathing hard when he got on the bed with her, naked . . .

In his room in the Cattleman's Club, Granville Stewart had gotten himself a different whore, one that suited him more than the skinny brunette. This one was blond, had more meat on her, and had a face that, while not beautiful, was at least pretty.

Her name was Lola, and she told him she was there to do whatever he wanted.

"Damn right you are, bitch," he said, "because I'm paying you."

"Yes, sir," she said, "you are."

"So get your clothes off."

She disrobed. Her body was opulent, with big breasts and wide hips.

"Turn around."

She turned around to show him her chunky butt. She was also older than the other girl, probably in her thirties, which didn't bother him because she was still about twenty years younger than him.

"Do you like me?" she asked, looking at him over her shoulder.

"You'll do," he said. "Now get my clothes off."

"Yes, sir."

She did as he asked, removed his clothes until he was naked. His penis was flaccid, which annoyed him.

"Get me hard, bitch!" he said, blaming her.

She took him in her hand, began stroking him, then had to work on him with her mouth before he actually started to get harder.

"That's it, bitch," he said, "now suck it good . . ."

* * *

Clint thought Evie had lovely skin. She was about thirty, not young by Western standards, but certainly still a young woman by what was becoming more modern standards. Gone were the days in the West when an unmarried girl of twenty was an old maid.

Evie's body was smooth and taut, her breasts firm and round, with lovely pink nipples that were extremely sensitive. Every time he touched them with his tongue, her body jerked, as if struck by lightning.

She lay on her back and allowed him to explore her body with his hands and mouth, and when she could bear it no longer, she fought him onto his back and started to return the favor.

She crawled all over him, rubbing her smooth skin and her hard nipples against him. When she got down to his hard cock, she rubbed it on her cheeks, pressed her lips to it, licked it, and finally took it into her mouth. As she sucked him, Clint reached down to touch her head tenderly, running his hands over her bare shoulders. She scratched his thighs, digging her nails in while she continued to suck him.

"Jesus," he said as he felt himself getting near an explosion he wasn't ready for yet. "Come on up here, girl, and sit on it!"

"My pleasure!" she said. She slid up on him, grabbing him with her hand, then held him still and sat down on him, taking him all the way inside.

"Oooh, yes," she said, and began to ride up and down on him . . .

Granville Stewart smacked Lola's bare butt again, adding to the redness that was already there.

"Ow!" she shouted.

"Shut up!"

He stuck his dick in her from behind, spreading her ass cheeks so he could get in. A whore in San Francisco had let him do this to her once and he'd loved it. Now whenever he bought a whore, he got her to do this. Even if he had to pay extra.

"Ow!" she said. "That h-hurts."

"Just relax," he said. "If you fight it, it'll hurt more. Just think about the extra money."

He started to move in and out of her, and while the pain didn't lessen, she tried to make him think that it did, hoping she'd get paid even more for that.

"There you go," he said, "that's good, ain't it?"

"Oh yeah, baby," she said, gritting her teeth, "that's real good."

She closed her eyes and a tear dripped from each one . . .

Evie leaned over, dangling her hard breasts in Clint's face. He reached out with his tongue for those marvelous nipples, then took them between his teeth and nibbled them. All that time Evie continued to ride him up and down, sliding easily on his slick cock. Clint could feel the sheet beneath him becoming soaked from her, but that only made him feel more excited by her.

He felt her begin to tremble atop him, and then suddenly she was jumping up and down on him rather than riding, and he did his best to stay with her . . .

TWENTY-FOUR

Granville Stewart woke up alone the next morning. After he'd finished with the whore, he'd sent her packing with her extra money. He smiled as he saw how gingerly she moved while dressing, and walking out the door. She'd remember him, all right.

He had to catch the stage in two hours, and wanted to get breakfast first. He wondered if Clint Adams and the newspaper girl, Loomis, would also be going back on the same stage. He also wondered if anyone at the Club had tried to hire Clint Adams to track rustlers.

Maybe, if Adams was on the stage, he'd talk to him this time.

Clint woke with Evie pressed tightly against him. He rolled away as gently as he could, so as not to wake her, then took the time to look at her while she slept. They had no top sheet on them because they had kicked it across the room.

She was lying on her side with her knees drawn up, moved slightly without waking. She may have been annoying, but she was very good in bed, so he could forgive her for a lot.

He leaned over and nibbled on one breast and then the other.

"Oooh," she said, grabbing his head and pushing his face into her breasts. "What a nice way to wake up."

She reached between them, trying to grab his penis, but he slipped away and got off the bed.

"Are you trying to play hard to get?"

"No," he said, "I'm hungry and I want breakfast before we get on the stage."

"Oh, we're going back together?"

He assumed that a ticket would be waiting for him whenever he wanted it. If not today, then the next stage. But he didn't see any reason not to return on today's stage.

"Looks like it."

She got on her knees, which succeeded in making her look very cute.

"Do you think Stewart will be on that stage?" she asked.

"I don't see why not," he said. "I think he's done here."

"I think we're all done here," she said.

"You better get back to your room and pack to leave," he said.

"I did that before I came here," she said with a grin.

Clint studied her, wondered if she had really been drunk when she came to his room, or if she'd been faking.

"Well, okay, then get back there and get dressed. We

can check out, and then go get some breakfast. You've made this trip before, I'm sure."

"I have."

"Then you know where to get some breakfast."

"I do," she said, leaping off the bed. "But are you sure you'd rather have food, when you could have this?" She spread her arms and posed.

He studied her beautiful, smooth skin, round breasts, pink nipples, and said, "It's a very close call, but yes, I want to eat."

She pouted at him and said, "You're a very mean man."

"You don't mean that."

"No, I don't," she said, putting on the clothes that had been strewn across the floor. "I'll meet you in the lobby."

"Ten minutes," he said.

She kissed him quickly, and left.

TWENTY-FIVE

The café where they ate breakfast was, as in Judith Gap, right across the street from the stage stop. It was not, however, as good as the place in Judith. But Evie warned Clint about that, so he ordered a simple bacon-and-egg plate. The coffee was weak, the eggs a bit runny, but the bacon was good.

Across the room from them sat Granville Stewart, working his way through a stack of flapjacks. They looked pretty good. Clint wondered if maybe he should have had that instead.

"What's the matter?" she asked.

"Stewart."

"What about him?"

"His breakfast looks better than mine."

"I warned you," she said. "Just have more bacon. Here, take mine."

"Okay."

"You're really gonna take it?"

"You offered it."

"Here," she said, "take one piece, leave me the other one."

She turned in her seat, looked around the room.

"See any other passengers?" Clint asked.

"No," she said. "I thought maybe the preacher and his wife would be on their way back."

"Why?"

"She didn't seem very happy," Evie said, "did she?"

"No. But the preacher seemed very determined."

"I thought she would win."

"We should have bet on it."

"So it'll only be the three on the stage," Clint said. "Think we'll be able to keep him quiet?"

She laughed.

"I'll bet we can keep him awake, though," she said.

"Think he'll get upset if we start to have sex?" Clint asked.

She laughed again.

"You're bad, Clint."

"We better get across the street," he said, pushing his plate away. "We want to get good seats."

"You're not gonna eat that piece of bacon, after all?" she asked.

"No," he said. "You can have it back."

She grabbed it and ate it as they went out the door.

"Is it because I touched it?" she asked.

"Yeah," he said, "I had my tongue all over you last night, but I won't eat your bacon because you touched it."

TWENTY-SIX

They got into the stagecoach first. Granville Stewart entered later. He sat across from Clint and Evie, while trying not to look at them.

The stage started moving and they were on their way back to Judith Gap.

After about half an hour Clint said, "Aw, come on, Stewart."

"I beg your pardon?" Stewart asked.

"You've got to talk to us sometime during this trip," Clint said.

"Why?"

"Because it's incredibly rude not to," Evie said.

Stewart looked at Evie. The look went on long enough for her to start squirming.

"I don't talk to reporters," he said finally.

"I don't either," Clint said, "but for this trip she's just a passenger, not a reporter."

"She's a woman," Stewart said.

"What's that got to do with anything?" she asked.

"Women are good for only one thing," the rancher said.

"And what's that?"

He grinned.

"Well, I'm not rude enough to come out and tell you," he said, leering at her, "but I'm sure you can figure it out."

Evie stared at him, then said, "You know what? Forget it. Don't talk to us."

She folded her arms and looked away.

Stewart found it funny.

"Whores," he said.

"What?" she said.

"Women. They're good as whores, and maybe waitresses and saloon girls, but that's about it."

"You sonofa—"

"That's enough, Stewart," Clint said.

"Why? You wanted me to talk."

"Well, not anymore. If you were trying to make us want you to shut up, you succeeded."

Granville Stewart looked out the window and said, "I always do."

The exchange convinced Clint that Stewart was a lot smarter than he'd first thought.

They managed to make the rest of the trip without talking. Clint and Evie took turns dozing off. Each time Clint woke up, he saw Stewart staring out the window. Apparently, he didn't sleep.

They pulled into Judith Gap, and Stewart was the first

one off the stage, opening the door even before the vehicle stopped.

"What a pig," Evie said.

"Even more than you first thought?"

"Oh yeah."

Clint got out of the stage and then helped Evie down. He caught her bag when the driver dropped it down.

"Here you go," Clint said.

"Thanks, Clint. I've got to go and see my editor. I'll see you later?"

"Yup, later."

He watched her walk away, then caught his saddlebags and rifle as the driver handed them down. Then he walked over to the sheriff's office.

"You're back," Piven said from his desk.

"Didn't you think I'd be back?" He put his saddlebags and rifle down on the man's desk. "Any coffee?"

"Help yourself."

"You want some?"

"Sure."

Clint poured two mugs full and carried them back to the desk. He pulled a chair over and sat down.

"So? What'd you find out?"

"Well," Clint said, "the cattlemen in this area are inept, except for Fredericks and Quarterman, and they're too old to do anything."

"And Stewart?"

"I'll get to him. I liked Sheriff Lewis, by the way. Nice guy."

"He's an old grouch."

"Yeah, I know, that's what I like about him."

"Do you meet the police chief?"

"Yes, I don't like him at all. He's going to make a mess of that police department."

"And what about Granville Stewart?"

"Well, a friend of mine thinks he's a pig."

"A friend of yours? Who?"

"Evie Loomis."

"Ah, Miss Loomis. So you and her are friends now, huh?"

"Kind of."

"And did you meet Stewart?"

"I did. And she's right," Clint said. "He is a pig. A smart pig."

"Smart?"

"He's got all those cattlemen wrapped around his finger," Clint said. "They're afraid of him, and they're afraid to do without him."

"So what'll they do?"

"Nothing," Clint said. "They tried to hire me, though."

"What?"

"The two old men," Clint said. "They thought I was looking for work. Like the old days."

"What'd you tell them?"

"To hire somebody else."

"You think they will?"

"Maybe."

"And Stewart?"

"He's going to do something smart."

"You were that impressed with him, huh?"

"Not as a man," Clint said. "He's rude, and he's got a low opinion of women. But I think he's a smart businessman."

"Well, when he gets back to his ranch, he's gonna be a mad businessman."

"Why? What happened?"

"While he was away, the rustlers hit."

"His place?"

"That's just it," Piven said. "They hit the three spreads around him."

"So? You think he's going to feel slighted?" Clint asked.

"Not slighted," Piven said. "He's gonna feet targeted."

"Targeted?"

"Yeah, he's gonna feel like the rustlers have painted a great big target around his place, with his house as the bull's-eye."

"You think he's going to feel that they're taunting him?"

"Yup."

"I'd like to see the look on his face when he gets home, then," Clint said. "I'd like to see him get mad."

"Why?"

Clint sipped his coffee and said, "He made the ride back very uncomfortable."

TWENTY-SEVEN

Stringer Jack watched Dutch Louie ride back into camp. By the time Louie had dismounted and walked over to the fire, Jack had finished one bowl of stew and was helping himself to another. Louie filled a bowl for himself, sat down, and started eating.

"He's back," Louie said.

"When?"

"Just now. Well, I mean a little while ago. I left town as soon as the stage pulled in."

"Anybody with him?"

"Just the reporter lady, and another man."

"Who?"

"I don't know. I never saw him before."

"And you didn't bother finding out who he was?"

"Well . . . you didn't tell me—"

"Never mind," Jack said. "Call California Ed over."

"Sure, boss."

Jack continued to eat until Louis came over with California Ed.

"What's up, boss?"

"A man got off the stage today with Granville Stewart. I wanna know who he is, and where he came from."

"Okay, boss."

"And do it quietly."

"Okay."

"Take somebody with you," Jack said, "but don't cause any trouble."

"Okay."

As Ed turned to leave, Jack said, "Wait."

"What?"

"Take Brocky with you. There was man on the stage when Brocky and the others tried to take it. Tell Brocky I wanna know if it's the same man."

"Okay, boss," Ed said. "I'll tell him."

Stringer Jack spooned more stew into his bowl.

Clint went back to his hotel and arranged for a bath. Piven wanted him to ride out to the Musselshell with him the next day, just for a look around. Today he was going to get a haircut, and a bath, and go and check on Eclipse to make sure he was okay.

He wondered if Piven was right about Stewart. Was the rancher going to get mad because the rustlers didn't hit him? It seemed an odd thought, but then Stewart seemed to be an odd man.

He was curious about what the man's next move would be.

* * *

Evie stopped off home first to get cleaned up and change, and then went to the office of the newspaper, *The Judith Page.*

"You're back," her editor, Lonny Beckham, said. "It's about time. You know nothin' gets done around here without you."

Beckham was in his seventies, but had more energy than two men half his age. They had more of a father-daughter relationship than a business one.

"Did you get anythin'?" he asked. "Somethin' on the cattlemen?"

"The cattlemen are a bunch of idiots," she said. "I've got something better."

"What's better than rustlers and cattlemen?" he asked.

"The Gunsmith."

"What?"

"Clint Adams came to town a couple of days ago, then took the stage with me to Helena."

"What for? What's he here for? Somebody hire him?"

"No, not hired," she said. "He's friends with Sheriff Piven."

"Is Piven gonna deputize him?"

"I don't think so."

"Whataya mean, you don't think so? Didn't you interview him?"

"He wouldn't be interviewed," she said, "yet."

"But you are gonna get an interview, right?"

"Lonny," she said, "I'm gonna get an interview if it kills me."

* * *

That night Clint answered his door with his gun in his hand again.

"It's just me," Evie said. She spread her hands. "I've had a bath."

"So have I."

"And a haircut," she said. "You look . . . cute. And you smell clean."

"So do you."

He pulled her into the room and kissed her.

TWENTY-EIGHT

California Ed and Brocky Gallagher didn't find out anything around town, not by just listening. They decided to go to the hotel and check the registration book quietly.

"I can't do that, sir," the clerk said when they asked to see it.

"Why not?"

"We have to protect our guests—"

Ed took out two bits, while Brocky took out his gun.

"Your choice."

The clerk took the two bits and pushed the book over to them.

"Read it," Ed said.

"I can't read, Ed," Brocky said.

Ed took the book and ran his finger down the names. When he came to the name *Clint Adams*, he stopped.

"Clint Adams," he said.

"The Gunsmith?" Brocky Gallagher said. "No wonder he was so good with a gun."

"Let's go."

They went outside the hotel, and across the street.

"We goin' back to camp?" Brocky asked.

"Nah, not yet," Ed said.

"Why not?"

"Jack's always sayin' he wants his boys to think for themselves," Ed said. "We're gonna wait for Clint Adams to come out. You're gonna make sure he's the one who was on the stage."

"And what if he sees me?"

"He won't. Just relax."

"Easy for you to say."

"Just watch the door."

Evie pressed her hands down on Clint's chest and rode his hard cock up and down slowly.

"Are you trying to kill me?" he asked.

"I'm trying . . . to make it . . . last," she said.

"Why?" he asked, grabbing her hips. "We'll just do it again."

"Clint—"

He flipped her over onto her back, popping out of her as he did so. He got between her legs and pushed himself in again all the way, making her catch her breath. She wrapped her legs around him and he began to fuck her faster and faster.

"Oh, yes," she said, "yes, yes, yes . . . that's it . . . ooh, God, yes . . ."

Clint grunted and exploded inside her with a low roar . . .

* * *

They did it again.

This time he spooned up against her, sliding his cock up between her soft thighs and inside her. Then he wrapped his arms around her so he could hold a breast with one hand, rubbing the nipple, and place the other hand between her legs. She gasped as he started to move in her, and manipulate her with his fingers.

"Jesus," she said, breathlessly, "now who's trying to kill who? Where did you learn this?"

"From a French woman," he said in her ear.

She laughed.

"Those poor French women," she said. "They get blamed for everything."

"On the contrary," he said, thrusting harder, "they get all the credit."

TWENTY-NINE

Granville Stewart received the news from his foreman when he arrived at home. He stood in his office and listened in stoic silence to the news.

"Sorry, boss," James Doubt said. "Maybe I shoulda waited until you got settled."

"No, Jim," Stewart said. "That's okay. How many head did they get?"

"Altogether? Maybe a couple of hundred. I don't get it. They coulda got more."

"They were just sending me a message," Stewart said.

"A message?"

"We're next," he said. "I'm sure of it."

"But . . . we'll be ready."

"You're damn right we will be," Stewart said.

"What happened in Helena?"

"Just what I thought would happen," Stewart said. "The bunch of idiots, they're runnin' around like chickens with their heads cut off. I laughed at them and left."

"What are they gonna do?"

"They'll probably try to hire the Gunsmith."

"The Gunsmith! How would they ever get ahold of him?" the foreman scoffed.

"He's in town," Stewart said. "Was in Helena, too. Now he's back here again."

"What's he doin' around here?" Doubt asked.

"I heard he's friends with Sheriff Piven," Stewart said. "Maybe he's going to help him track the rustlers."

"Nat could use some help," Doubt said, "but Clint won't wear a badge."

Stewart frowned.

"Clint? You know him?'

"Yeah," Doubt said, "met him back when I was wearin' a badge in the Dakotas."

"How long ago was that?"

"I don't know. Gotta be fifteen years."

"Would he remember you?"

"Sure he would."

"Okay," Stewart said. "Tomorrow you go into town and accidentally bump into him."

"What for?"

"Find out what's on his mind," Stewart said. "Somebody in Helena must have offered him a lot of money. I want to know if he took it, or he's just hanging around like you said, to help Piven."

"Why don't you ask him?"

"Because me and him didn't get along, that's why. I want you to do it."

"Okay, boss," Doubt said.

"Put Tucker in charge of the boys while you're away."

"Tucker, huh?" Doubt asked. "You wouldn't be groomin' him for my job, would ya?"

"Your job's your job as long as you want it, Jim," Stewart said.

"I appreciate that, boss."

"Okay, Jim. You can go."

"Thanks, boss."

After his foreman left, Granville Stewart sat down behind his desk. He did some paperwork before deciding he ought to wash up and get changed from his stage ride.

He smiled as he left the office, remembering the look on the newspaperwoman's face when he told her all women were whores. He moved through the house, took the stairs, and by the time he walked into his bedroom, he was laughing out loud.

Jim Doubt had worn a badge for about twelve years. He was right in the middle of that time when he ran into Clint Adams. Adams had come to town—Decatur, South Dakota, it was—looking for a man. He and Doubt ended up working together, tracking him down. Doubt had expected Adams to kill the man when they found him, but he didn't. He brought him in alive.

He went out to the bunkhouse to tell Tucker about taking over the next day.

"What are you up to?" Tucker asked.

"Just goin' to town," Doubt said. "To see an old friend."

"Be back tomorrow night?"

"Sure, I'll be back."

He went to his own room, in the same building but separate from the others. He'd been working for Granville Stewart for five years. He knew a lot of people didn't like the man, but he did.

He took off his boots and sat on his hard bunk. He had a book on the table next to the bed, Mark Twain. It had been Clint Adams who'd introduced him to Twain's writings.

Whatever was going to happen, he hoped he wouldn't have to choose between Clint Adams and Granville Stewart.

THIRTY

California Ed and Brocky Gallagher stayed in the doorway across from the hotel all night.

"This is what you meant about thinkin' for ourselves?" Gallagher asked. "Sleepin' standin' up?"

"I ain't about to go back to camp without the information Jack wants, are you?"

"Well, no."

"There," Ed said. "They're comin' out."

Across the street Clint and Evie came out of the hotel and turned right.

"That him?" Ed asked. "That the guy on the stage?"

"That's him."

"Okay," Ed said, "let's go."

"Back to camp?"

"After we talk to the desk clerk."

Clint had breakfast with Evie, same place they'd had it the first time, across from the stage office.

"I told my editor about you," she said.

"All about me?" he asked with a grin.

"No," she said, "only the parts he needed to know."

"And what parts were they?"

"Just that you were in Helena, and you're here."

"And he wants you to interview me, right?"

"Well, yeah," she said. "What newspaper wouldn't want an interview with Clint Adams?"

"I'm not here to be interviewed."

"I know that. You're here to help your friend, the sheriff."

"That's right. Why don't you write about Nat Piven. He's a good lawman."

"I know it," she said. "I've written about Nat quite a few times."

"What about the rustlers? Have you written about them?"

"My editor's done a couple of editorials about rustling, but it's hard to write about somebody you don't know."

"Who's your editor?"

"Why? You think you'll recognize his name?"

"Probably not."

"It's Lonny, Lonny Beckham."

"What's he like?"

"Like a father to me."

"Anybody else work at the paper?"

"Nope, just him and me. He also runs the press."

"No boyfriends in town?"

"No," she said, "don't worry. You won't have to fight anybody for me."

"Well, that's good."

At that point the door opened and Nat Piven came in.

"There's the sheriff," she said, turning her head. "Do you want to invite him to join us? It's all right with me."

"Sure, why not?" Clint waved to Piven and the man came over.

"Join us for breakfast, Nat?"

"Sure."

He sat and the waitress came over and took his order, poured him some coffee.

"Are you getting' anythin' out of him, Evie?" Piven asked.

"Not much," she said. "He won't give me an interview. He's gonna get me in trouble with Lonny. He's gonna get me fired. You tell him, Nat."

"Lonny's got no paper without you, Evie, you know that."

"Yeah, but you didn't have to tell him that," she said. She took her napkin from her lap and put it on the table. "I have to get to work. You can keep Clint company while he finishes his breakfast." She took the last piece of bacon from her ate and put it on Clint's, next to his steak. "I'll see you both later."

They both watched her go out the door, and then the waitress appeared with Piven's ham and eggs and he dug in.

THIRTY-ONE

California Ed and Brocky Gallagher had waited until Clint and Evie were out of sight then crossed over to the hotel.

They crossed the floor to the desk and the clerk looked startled when he saw them.

"Yes?"

"The man who just left," Ed said. "The one with the woman."

"What about him?"

"Was that Clint Adams?"

"I'm not supposed to give information—"

Gallagher touched his gun and asked, "Are we gonna go through this again?"

"N-No," the clerk said. "I—I'll tell you. That was Clint Adams who just left."

"Okay," Ed said, turning to face Gallagher. "Now we go back to camp."

* * *

"You're not in love with her, are you, Nat?" Clint asked.

"Sure," Piven said, "and so is every other man in town. She's also kind of our little sister, so you be careful with her, Clint."

"What's on your agenda for today?" Clint asked.

"Me? I thought I'd go and talk to Stewart."

"Why?"

"Maybe find out what he's plannin'."

"What about the other ranchers?"

"I already talked to three whose spreads got hit," he said. "They don't know nothin', didn't see nothin'."

"They lose any men?"

"No," Piven said. "A couple got hurt, but nobody got killed."

"I wonder if the rustlers are being careful not to kill anyone," Clint said, "or if they just haven't yet."

"My money's on 'haven't yet,'" Piven said. "Sooner or later, they'll have to."

"When that happens, maybe you can bring in some federal help."

"Maybe. For now I'll just ride out to see Stewart today, see what he has to say. You wanna come with me?"

"Actually, no. I'll wait until you go out and ride the river, then I'll go with you."

"Okay."

Clint picked up Evie's piece of bacon and ate it.

When they left the café, a man was riding into town.

"I know that man," Clint said.

"Do you? That's Jim Doubt."

"Sure, I knew him in the Dakotas. He was a lawman. Oh, about ten or twelve years ago."

"Well, these days," Piven said, "he's Granville Stewart's foreman."

"Well," Clint said, "what do you know about that?"

THIRTY-TWO

Clint stepped into the street as Jim Doubt rode up even with him.

Doubt, for his part, had been wondering how to find Clint Adams, when suddenly he appeared in the street. And he had a smile on his face.

"Jim Doubt, as I live and breathe."

"Clint Adams," Doubt said. "Jesus." He dismounted and the two men shook hands. "How long's it been?"

"Ten, twelve years," Clint said. "I hear you got yourself a good job. Smart man to stop wearing a badge."

"I beg your pardon?" Sheriff Piven said.

"Hey, Sheriff," Doubt said. "He didn't mean nothin' by that. He's just the kinda guy doesn't like to wear a badge himself."

"What about you?" Clint asked. "You did give it up, right?"

"When somethin' better came along, yeah."

"Granville Stewart."

"That's right," Doubt said. "He's a good man. And a good boss."

"Glad to hear it," Clint said. "Where were you headed, Jim?"

"Just came to town to get a drink," Doubt said. "Wanna join me?"

"This early? I just had breakfast."

"That's okay," Doubt said. "Honey's opens early every day."

"Okay, then why not?" Clint turned to Piven. "Nat?"

"I got rounds," Piven said, "but if you're still there later, sure."

"Okay, then," Clint said. "Let's walk over."

Ed and Brocky Gallagher went to the livery, where they'd left their mounts. They saddled up, and rode out of town to return to Stringer Jack's camp.

Doubt tied his horse off outside Honey's Saloon. They went inside. It was early, and while there were customers in the place, it was too early for it to be busy. They had their pick of places at the bar.

"Beer?" Doubt asked Clint. "I'll buy the first round."

"Okay."

"Two beers," Doubt said to one of the bartenders.

"Comin' up."

When they each had a cold mug in their hands, Doubt said, "So what brings you to Judith Gap?"

"I'm sure your boss probably told you," Clint said.

"He hardly tells me anythin'," Doubt that. "At least, nothin' I don't need to know. He came back from Helena and told me I could have some time to come to town and have a drink."

"He didn't tell you to come into town and see what was on my mind?" Clint asked.

"What? No, I told you. I just came into town for a beer." Doubt held his mug up. "And I ran into an old friend."

"Well then," Clint said, "fill me in on twelve years."

"That's gonna be boring," Doubt said. "And I don't need to be filled in about you."

"All you've probably heard is my reputation," Clint said.

"And if half of it is true . . ." Doubt said.

"Less than that probably."

"That's still pretty impressive," Doubt said. "In fact, you're rep was impressive back then. So were you. It seems like it's just continued to grow."

"What about you?" Clint asked. "Are you happy being a ranch foreman?"

"Sure," Doubt said. "I report only to Stewart, and I get paid a good salary. Yeah, I guess I'm pretty happy where I am."

"How do you feel about the rustlers?"

"They haven't touched any of our stock yet."

"Will your boss wait until they do before he takes action?"

"Like I said, Clint," Doubt replied, "I don't know what he's thinkin' until he tells me."

"Well, what would you do?"

"Since they hit the spreads all around us," Doubt said, "I'd take my men and go huntin' for them."

"So why didn't you?" Clint asked. "I mean, while your boss was in Helena."

"I had orders not to make a move unless they actually hit our stock."

"How do your men feel?"

"They'll go along with whatever Stewart wants. You think I'm the only one happy with my job? He pays his men twice what the other spreads pay theirs."

"So they'll do whatever he wants them to do?"

"That's right."

Clint sipped his beer, looked at a couple of the girls who came to the bar for drinks. Honey's sure had its own rules, opening early and having girls work the floor while some people were still having breakfast elsewhere.

"I was in Helena when he went to the Cattleman's Club."

"That so? Did you hear the meetin'?"

Clint nodded. "It wasn't much of a meeting," he said. "He pretty much told the others they were idiots, and they were on their own."

"That sounds like my boss."

"They're comin' back, boss," Red Mike said.

"I see 'em," Stringer Jack said.

He poured himself a cup of coffee, then stepped forward to meet his men.

As they dismounted, he said, "I didn't expect you to be gone all night."

"We wanted to make sure we came back with the information you wanted, boss," California Ed said.

"And did you?"

"Yeah, we did," Ed said. "Brocky says the man from the stagecoach is Clint Adams, all right."

"Okay," Stringer Jack said. "So now we know we may have to deal with the Gunsmith."

"And that's bad?" Ed asked. "Ain't it?"

"We'll have to wait and see."

THIRTY-THREE

Clint and Doubt eventually moved to a table and started to allow the saloon girls to bring them their drinks. Doubt was very happy with the attention, and had either one girl or the other on his lap the whole time.

The batwings opened and the sheriff stepped in. He looked around, spotted Clint and Doubt, and waved. He went to the bar, got himself a beer, and joined them.

"Hey, Katy," he said to the blonde on Doubt's lap.

"Hello, Sheriff."

"Do me a favor, will you? Go serve somebody a drink."

"Sure." She kissed Doubt on the cheek and left.

"I hope you had a good reason for that," the foreman said to the lawman.

"What's going on, Nat?" Clint asked.

"I just came from your hotel."

"And?"

"The clerk was kind of worked up," he said. "Two men threatened him, and asked questions about you."

"What kind of questions?"

"Well, apparently they watched you leave this morning, then went in and asked the clerk if you were . . . well, you."

"They're trying to identify me," Clint said. "I thought I was being watched, but I didn't pay it much attention. I'll bet the rustlers sent the one who got away into town to identify me."

"So what?" Doubt asked. "Now they know they have to deal with the Gunsmith."

"That might not have the effect you think," Piven said.

"Whataya mean?" Doubt asked.

"Knowing that the Gunsmith is in the area might urge them into action," Clint said. "That's what he means. They may take it as a challenge."

"Maybe," Piven said, "the rustlers will move and we'll get a look at them."

"You still going to see Granville Stewart today?" Clint asked.

"I think maybe you and me should ride out to the river," Piven said. "Maybe we'll be able to see somethin' stirrin' out there."

"Like rustlers?" Doubt asked.

"Maybe."

"You mind if I tag along?"

"You don't think your boss will mind you riding along?" Clint asked.

"Hell," Doubt said, "he told me to take some time off. How about I don't even tell him?"

"We'll probably be back late. You're going to spend the night in town?" Clint asked.

"Maybe I'll sleep on some hay in the livery," Doubt said.

"Or you can have the floor in my room."

"Sure, why not? I got a bedroll on my saddle." He looked at Piven. "Sheriff?"

"Why not?" Piven said. "The more the merrier. You can handle a gun, can't you?"

Doubt looked at Clint and smiled.

"He could twelve years ago," Clint said.

"Even better now," Doubt said.

"Good." Piven finished his beer. "Why don't we meet in front of the livery in an hour?"

"I'll be there," Doubt said. "Be nice to get out in the open without having to ride ramrod over some lazy bastards. And the cows, and horses, too."

THIRTY-FOUR

Clint left the saloon, squinting at the sunlight. Usually when he came out of a saloon, it wasn't quite so bright. It felt odd for it to still be so early in the day.

He knew the general direction of the newspaper office, so he headed that way. Within a few blocks he came to it. He stopped and looked in the window. An older man was working at the press, while Evie was seated in an inner office at a desk, probably working on a story.

He opened the door and walked in.

"Help you?" the man asked.

Clint assumed this was Lonny Beckham.

"I'm looking for Evie."

"You Adams?"

"That's right."

"You come to give my girl an interview?"

"Not really."

"Why not?"

"I don't do interviews."

"Seems I mighta seen an interview a time or two over the years."

"Then maybe I should say I don't do them anymore."

"Well, go ahead and talk to Evie, then," Beckham said. "But don't keep her too long. She's got work to do."

"Yes, sir."

Clint went to the door of the office and knocked. Evie turned, smiled, and waved him in.

"Couldn't stay away from me, huh?" she said as he entered.

"I wanted to see where you worked."

"Well, this is it," she said, spreading her arms. "Where I do all my writing."

"What are you working on now?" he asked.

"I'll never tell," she said. "You'll have to wait to read it."

"So what really brings you over here?"

He turned and looked at Lonny, who was still working on the press.

"I wanted to tell you that I'll have somebody in my room tonight."

"You found another girl already?"

"There are other girls in town?" he asked.

"Like you haven't been to Honey's and seen all those beautiful saloon girls," she said.

"Oh, them," he said. "Well, it's none of them. It's an old friend of mine, Jim Doubt."

"Doubt? Granville Stewart's foreman?"

"Turns out I knew him about twelve years ago," Clint said. "We had a drink to catch up and he was around when the sheriff said he wanted to go out and ride along the river later today. So, he's going to go with us, which means he'll spend the night in town. On a bedroll on my floor."

"Well," she said, "you could give him your bed and come spend the night at my place."

"That's a thought."

He reached for her, but she backed away and wagged her finger at him.

"Not in front of Lonny," she warned. "I told you he's like a father to me. He thinks I'm a virgin."

"Well, we don't want to disappoint him," he said. "You'll have to tell me where you live."

"I'll do better than that," she said. "I'll show it to you, right after you buy me dinner tonight."

"You got a deal," Clint said. "I'll come by here and get you later."

"At five," she said.

"See you then."

He went back past the press and got a dirty look from Lonny Beckham.

Stringer Jack took a long drink from a bottle of whiskey he kept in his tent, and then stepped outside. He called Frank Hanson over.

"Get the men over here."

"Where we goin', boss?"

"I think it's time to pay a visit to the DHS spread."

"We finally gonna hit Stewart's place, huh?" Hanson asked. "When?"

"Just get the men over here and I'll tell everybody at the same time."

"Okay, boss."

Jack was going to take his gang over to Granville

Stewart's spread and pick out a few hundred head of prime stock. Maybe that would bring the Gunsmith out of Judith Gap and into the basin looking for trouble.

The men started to gather round him and he got himself a cup of coffee and then gave them the news.

"Boys, tomorrow we hit the big time," he said. "We're gonna hit the biggest spread in the Basin, and then we're gonna get a shot at the biggest gun in the West."

THIRTY-FIVE

When Clint got to the livery, he found both the sheriff and Jim Doubt saddling their horses.

"We would've saddled your horse for you, but that big beast won't let anybody near him."

"He's got a taste for fingers," Clint said. "Strangers' fingers."

"Good-lookin' animal, though," Doubt said.

"Thanks."

They all got their mounts saddled and walked them outside.

"We'll take our time," Sheriff Piven said. "There's no point in pushing the horses. The river'll be there when we get there."

They mounted up and rode out.

Stringer Jack watched his boys mount up. He had about twelve men. He'd had more, but Clint Adams had killed some of them when he was on the stage.

He studied his men. California Ed, Dutch Louie, Red Mike, Brocky Gallagher, Silas Nickerson, Bill Williams, Paddy Rose, Swift Bill, Dixie Burr, Orville Edwards, and Frank Hanson.

They were all good boys, as long as they had somebody leading them. There wasn't any of them who'd be able to run a gang of their own. That was okay with Jack. Although he would have liked a few of them to use their heads sometimes, he didn't have to worry about any of them trying to take over the gang. He trusted them. That was important when you led your own gang.

Frank Hanson came over.

"The men are all mounted, Jack," he said.

"Okay, Frank. Get me my horse, will you?"

"Sure, boss."

Hanson walked Stringer Jack's roan over to him, and Jack mounted.

"Okay, men," Jack said, "today's the day we make our mark, and I want you to remember one thing. Nobody shoot until I do, but when we do start shooting, shoot to kill."

THIRTY-SIX

"A hundred yards wide," Sheriff Nat Piven said, "but only about three feet deep. We could pretty much ride across at any point. Also, it's pretty much used by all the spreads to water their stock."

"Which means rustlers know exactly where to find that stock," Clint said.

"We guard ours pretty good," Jim Doubt said. "Most of our men can use a gun pretty good."

"How many men on guard at a time?" Clint asked.

"Three, maybe four," Doubt said. "Each. We got cattle, and horses."

"So your forces are split, then."

"I guess you could look at it that way," Doubt said with a frown.

"Up ahead is the Bar-Q spread," Piven said. "Let's make a stop there."

"Quentin Jones's spread," Doubt said. "They got hit two days ago."

"You said you talked to all the spreads that got hit," Clint said.

"Maybe you'll think of somethin' to ask that I didn't."

"Maybe," Clint said.

"No harm in stoppin' to see them again," Piven said.

"Okay."

They came upon a couple of riders who looked to be rounding up strays.

"That's Jeffers, the foreman of the Bar-Q," Doubt said.

"You talk to him, Sheriff?" Clint asked.

"I talked to Quint Jones, his boss," Piven said. "Not him."

"He's a good ol' boy," Doubt said, "but let's make sure he sees your badge so he don't shoot at us before we reach him."

"That's one of the nice things about the sun reflectin' off this tin," Piven said.

They started to ride over to where the Bar-Q boys were sitting. Sure enough, the sun reflected off the tin on Piven's chest, announcing their arrival.

"Hey, Jeff!" Doubt called out.

"That you, Jim? With the law?"

"That's right."

Jeffers and his man still looked ready to draw as they got closer.

"Who's that with ya?" Jeffers asked.

"This is a friend of mine," Doubt said. "You might know him. Clint Adams?"

"The Gunsmith?"

"That's right."

"Keep comin'." Jeffers waved, relaxing a bit.

Clint, Piven, and Doubt rode right up on the two men, and the two foremen reached over and shook hands.

"Sheriff," Jeffers said with a nod.

"Jeffers."

"What's the Gunsmith goin' hereabouts?" he asked, looking at Clint.

"I happen to be friends with both these gents," Clint said. "The sheriff asked me to come to Judith Gap to help him out, and I ran into Jim last night."

Jeffers finally extended his hand and Clint shook it.

"This is my man, Ben Maple."

They all nodded at each other.

Jeffers was about the same age as Doubt, early forties, but while Doubt was clean shaven, Jeffers sported a bushy mustache. The Bar-Q hand, Maple, was in his thirties, with some heavy stubble on his face.

"What brings you boys out here?"

"Wanted to take a look around," Piven said. "Maybe talk to some of your boys, some of the hands from the other spreads who got hit. See if anybody saw anything."

"We didn't see a thing," Jeffers said. "Maple and I weren't with the herd when they hit. They ambushed my boys, managed to get the herd from 'em without killin' anybody, which I guess is some kinda good news."

"Dependin' on how ya look at it," Maple said.

"How do you mean?" Clint asked.

"He's talkin' about my boss thinkin' his men shoulda died to save his herd," Jeffers said.

"You don't feel that way?" Piven asked.

"This is a job," Jeffers said. "I ain't gonna die for a job."

"I see your point," Doubt agreed.

"What brings you out here?" Piven asked.

"Looks like the rustlers ain't so good at being cow-pokes," Maple said. "Some of the herd got away from them, and we been pickin' 'em up."

THIRTY-SEVEN

They moved along, met riders from the other spreads who had been rustled. They got the same story everywhere. Nobody had seen anything. The rustlers had struck swiftly, and effectively. They had a good leader.

They stopped midafternoon to rest the horses, share some water and beef jerky.

"Whoever this guy is," Clint said, "the leader, apparently he's smart."

"How many smart rustlers are there?" Doubt asked. "In my experience they're usually not that smart, and do somethin' stupid to get caught."

"Well then," Piven said, "they may be about to do that, now that they know Clint's here. This smart man might want to challenge the Gunsmith."

"My luck," Clint said. "If he wants to challenge me, why doesn't he just call me out in the street? At least I know where I stand with that."

"You tracked rustlers before," Piven said.

"You've tracked men before, period," Doubt said. "That's how we met."

"Yeah, yeah," Clint said. "But I need a trail before I can track."

"We need them to hit again," Piven said, "so we'll have a fresh trail."

"I guess we better be careful what we wish for," Clint said.

Stringer Jack looked down at the DHS spread in front of him. Fine-looking cattle, hundreds of head in this particular herd. He knew that Granville Stewart had thousands of head, but didn't keep them altogether in one place. That was a smart thing to do. However, it did split up his men. There were three men watching these particular cattle.

"Frank, take half the men, circle around to the other side."

"Right."

"Don't make a move until I do."

"Right, boss."

He turned, picked out California Ed.

"Stay here with the rest of the men."

"Okay."

"I'm gonna ride down," he said, "and see if I can talk some sense into them. If I signal, you ride down and you come shootin'. Understand?"

"Yeah, boss."

Stringer Jack nodded, turned his roan, and started down the hill.

Dave Donovan saw the rider coming down the hill toward them. He called out to the other men.

"Hey!" He pointed at the approaching rider. Both men, Harry Sands and Eli Watts, nodded that they also saw him, but they remained where they were positioned.

The rider rode toward the herd and headed straight for Donovan.

"That's far enough," Donovan said, holding his rifle ready.

"Whataya mean?" Stringer Jack asked.

"What's your business here?" Donovan asked.

Jack looked around.

"Only three of you here, huh?"

"It's enough."

"You sure? I heard you been having trouble with rustlers around here."

"Not us," Donovan said. "Not the DHS. Nobody'd dare hit Mr. Stewart's herd. Nobody in their right mind anyway."

"Granville Stewart's herd, huh?"

"That's right."

"Well, believe it or not," Stringer Jack said, leaning on his saddle horn, "I'm here to help you and your two friends."

"That so?"

"Yeah, it is."

"Help us what?"

"Well," Jack said. "Help you stay alive."

"What now?" Doubt asked as they mounted up again.

"I'd like to see your stock, Jim."

"We got 'em split up, so nobody could ever hit the whole herd," Doubt said, "but I'd need my boss's okay to show you."

"Why don't we go on to your place, then?" Piven said. "Check in with your men, maybe even talk to your boss, like I planned to before. And get his okay."

"Suits me," Doubt said.

"Me, too," Clint said. "I'd like to see how Stewart is taking the news of his neighbors being hit."

Doubt looked over at Clint.

"You ain't gonna see nothin'," Doubt told him. "He keeps everythin' inside."

"I guess I'll see for myself."

THIRTY-EIGHT

Clint, Piven, and Doubt rode up to the DHS spread. Clint was impressed by the sheer size of the house, not to mention the barn and corral.

Several men came walking over to them. Clint wondered why they weren't out with the herds. What was there here at the house to guard?

"Hey, boss," one of them said to Doubt. "What gives?"

"I was in town when the sheriff said he was gonna ride out to see Mr. Stewart. I decided to come along."

"Who's this other fella?" someone else asked.

"Friend of mine," Doubt said. "Boys, meet Clint Adams."

Clint could see that they all recognized the name, but none of them said anything.

"Where's the boss?" Doubt asked.

"He's inside."

Doubt looked at Piven and Clint.

"I'll go and get him."

He handed his reins to Clint and dismounted. They watched him go up the steps and into the house. Clint had seen many large ranches like this—well, not quite like this. Unfortunately, the people who lived in homes like this usually developed an attitude of . . . superiority. And he'd already seen that in Granville Stewart.

The door to the house opened and Doubt came out, followed by Granville Stewart. Piven and Clint remained mounted, so the two men came down the steps to them.

"What brings you gents out to my place?" he asked.

"Mr. Stewart, we figure it won't be long before the rustlers hit you. After all, they've hit everybody around you."

"So what? That just means they know better than to come after my stock."

"We don't think that's true," Clint said, "and neither do you."

Stewart gave Jim Doubt a long look. The foreman looked away.

"Mr. Stewart, we want your permission for Jim to take us around to check on your herd."

Stewart frowned, but said, "Guess I can't exactly complain that the law's looking to help me, can I, Sheriff?"

"I wouldn't think so, sir."

"Okay, then," Stewart said. "Jim, take them around. Show them our stock."

"Sure, boss."

Doubt mounted his horse.

"Then bring them back here," Stewart continued. "Bring them inside for a glass of brandy."

"Right, boss."

"Thank you, Mr. Stewart."

"No, Sheriff, thank you."

The three men wheeled their horses about and rode back the way they had come.

"I don't know what you mean," Donovan said to Stringer Jack.

"Well, the three of you work for Granville Stewart," Jack said.

"So?"

"These are his cows."

"That's right."

"Are the three of you ready to die protectin' these cows?"

"What?" Donovan held his rifle tightly.

"I've got men all around you, friend," Stringer Jack said.

Donovan looked around, didn't see anyone.

"You can't see 'em, but all I have to do is raise my hands, and they'll be here."

Donovan licked his lips.

"Whatayou want?"

"I want you and your friends to just ride away," Jack said. "Just go, and nobody gets hurt."

"We can't do that."

"Why? These cattle don't belong to you. Why die for them?"

Donovan nervously licked his lips again, and swallowed.

"Why don't you call your partners over and let them in on the decision," Jack said. "I don't think they want you to decide life or death for them, do you?"

Donovan looked at Jack for a few moments, wondering who this fella was, and then waved at his compadres to ride over.

"You lay it out for them, friend," Stringer Jack said, "and then you can all make your decision."

THIRTY-NINE

They heard the shots.

"Where's that coming from?" Doubt said.

Piven stood in his stirrups and listened.

It was a quick volley of shots, and then it stopped.

"That way," Clint said, pointing. "Come on."

He rode off with Piven and Doubt behind him.

Clint, riding Eclipse, came upon the scene well before the other two. He saw three men lying on the ground, no horses anywhere. The ground was churned up and there had obviously been a herd of cattle there very recently. This was clearly the spot Doubt had been taking them to.

They had already ridden to other places where herd were being guarded by three and four men. This was to be the third place they checked, but obviously they were too late.

When Piven and Doubt arrived, Clint had dismounted and was checking the bodies.

"What the hell—" Doubt said, gaping at the men on the ground.

He and Piven dismounted.

"They're dead, Jim," Clint told him.

"Jesus."

Doubt went to each body in turn. Clint walked over to stand next to Piven.

"Looks like they crossed the line this time," he said. "Killed three men."

"Took the herd, and their horses," Piven said. "Looks like we got what we asked for, Clint. A fresh trail to follow."

Doubt walked away from the bodies and joined Clint and Piven.

"We better get started," Piven said. "They're driving a herd of . . . how many?"

"A couple of hundred," Doubt said tonelessly.

"A couple of hundred head should slow them down enough for us to catch up to them."

"I'm goin' back," Doubt said.

"What?" Piven asked.

"Back to the ranch," he said. "I'm gonna get the boss and my men and come back here. Then we'll catch up to you."

"But if we go now—" Piven said.

"These are my men," Doubt said. "They have to be buried. You and Clint go ahead, start trackin'. If the leader of these rustlers is as smart as you think he is, he won't even be with the herd when you catch up."

Doubt walked to his horse and mounted.

"We'll catch up," he said, "and we'll make them pay."

He turned his horse and galloped off.

Clint walked around the scene while Piven mounted his horse and held Eclipse's reins.

"Can you tell how many?"

Clint walked back, took Eclipse's reins, and mounted up.

"The ground's pretty beat up, but I'd think there were a dozen or more."

"If we had time, I'd wait for Doubt and the ranch hands," Piven said. "I don't like doin' this with only two of us."

"We can track them, Nat, and wait for the hands to catch up before we take them."

"Yeah, we can do that," Piven said. "All right, Clint. Lead off, then."

"Looks like they're headed for the river."

Jim Doubt rode up to the DHS Ranch and dismounted frantically. The men came running over.

"Get mounted up!" he yelled. "I want everybody armed and ready to go in five minutes. You got that? Five minutes!"

"What's goin' on—"

"Just do it!"

Shouting was not Jim Doubt's usual way to giving orders. The men were galvanized into action, ran for their guns and their horses.

Doubt rushed up the steps and into the house, slamming the door open.

"Boss!" he shouted. "Granville!"

Stewart came rushing out of his office.

"What the hell—"

"We been hit," Doubt said. "They killed Donovan, Sands, and Watts and took two hundred head."

Stewart pointed his finger at Doubt.

"Get the men ready."

"They'll be armed and mounted in three minutes."

"I'll be right out."

Doubt left the house, watched as the men gathered there.

FORTY

Clint and Piven followed the plain trail left by two hundred head of cattle and at least twelve horsemen.

They drove the cattle across the river, and then headed north, away from Judith Gap and into the Judith Basin in the Bitterroot Valley.

"They're taking these cattle to wherever they've got the others stashed," Clint guessed. "How many head did you say they took from the other spreads?"

"Probably as many as they took today."

"Where could they hide four hundred head of cattle?" Clint asked.

"There's any number of valleys or canyons they could be using."

"Make an educated guess," Clint said.

"You'd do better to get a guess from your friend Doubt, or even Stewart," Piven said. "I'm usually in town, Clint."

"Okay," Clint said, "I guess we'll have to wait for them to catch up."

•

They went a few more miles and stopped.

"What?" Piven asked.

"They split the herd," Clint said.

"How many times?"

"Looks like they split it into three."

"Great, and there's two of us."

Piven stood in his stirrups and looked behind them. There was no sign of Granville Stewart and his men.

"Whataya wanna do?" Piven asked.

"Split up, keep tracking," Clint said. "We just need to locate some of them, some of the herd. Then we can move in and take them, and find the rest of them. Find out who the leader is."

Piven looked behind him again.

"You think Stewart is going to have anybody with him who can read sign and track?" the sheriff asked.

"Yeah, Jim Doubt can track. Not as good as me, but he can do it."

"Well then, let's hope they'll follow the third group that way," Clint said, pointing, "and not one of us."

"Can't we leave them a . . . message somehow?"

"Sure."

Clint dismounted, collected a bunch of stones, and made a crude arrow on the ground. Then he mounted up.

"I'll go this way, you go that way, and hopefully your boss will go that way."

"Okay. But remember, you don't have a badge. When you spot them, just follow. When they settle in, come back right here to this arrow and meet me."

"Got it."

"Good luck."

"You, too."

When Doubt saw the stone arrow in the ground, he called a halt to their progress.

"What?" Granville Stewart asked.

Doubt pointed.

"What the hell—"

Doubt studied the ground.

"They split the herd here," he said. "Clint went one way, and Sheriff Piven another. They want us to go that way."

"How do we know the rustlers didn't put that stone arrow in the ground to get us to go the wrong way?" Stewart asked.

"Because years ago Clint used that same trick to direct me."

"You and Adams renew your friendship?"

"Sort of."

"Don't forget where your loyalty lies, Jim," Stewart said.

"Why would my loyalties have to divide?" Doubt asked. "Ain't we all after the same thing?"

"I guess we'll have to see," Stewart said. "So you think we should go that way?"

"Yeah," Doubt said. "Somebody definitely drove some cattle that way."

"Okay," Stewart said, "lead the way."

Red Mike and Brocky Gallagher drove their cattle into the corral they'd built at Bates Point, near the Musselshell.

"What about the horses?" Gallagher asked.

There were several horses in another small corral, which Stringer Jack did not know they had.

"We'll have to sell them," Red Mike said. "If Jack comes here and finds them, he'll kill us."

"When should we move 'em?" Brocky asked.

"Now, I guess," Red Mike said. "Right now."

FORTY-ONE

It was Jim Doubt, Granville Stewart, and the DHS boys who followed Red Mike and Brocky Gallagher to Rocky Point. They looked down on the site from a point above it.

"I never thought of this," Doubt said. "Rocky Point is a good place to hide a large number of cattle or horses."

"Those are our cattle, all right," Stewart said. "You see anybody around?"

"No," Doubt said, "but let's be careful."

There were two corrals, a larger and smaller one, and a small shack.

"We need somebody to sneak down there and get a look inside that shack," Doubt said.

"I'll do it, boss," one of the men said. His name was Taylor, and he'd been with the DHS for three years. Doubt trusted him with almost any kind of job.

"Okay," Doubt said, "but be careful. We don't want them to start shootin', because then we'd have to shoot back. We want at least one of them alive."

"I'll keep that in mind," Taylor said, and dismounted. He started to work his way down to the shack on foot.

Clint tracked three rustlers and their part of the herd to a box canyon, where all they had to do was construct a gate to keep the cows in.

There were only three, so he rode up on them confidently.

Dutch Louie, Orville Edwards, and Bill Williams drove the cattle into the box and closed the gate. When they started congratulating each other, Dutch noticed the man riding toward them.

"We got company."

The three men turned to face Clint Adams.

Stringer Jack returned to Bates Point with Frank Hanson, Silas Nickerson, Paddy Rose, and California Ed. Old Man James and his two sons were still there. That made seven of them. The rest of the men were hiding the cows they'd stolen.

Old Man James came out to greet them.

"You know when Granville Stewart finds out what you've done, he'll come after us," the old man said.

"We'll be ready," Jack said.

Dixie Burr and Swift Bill watched as Sheriff Nat Piven rode up on them. Behind them the stolen cows stirred inside a corral.

"Damn it," Burr said. "The law."

"How'd he find us?" Bill asked.

"It don't matter," Burr said. "We got to kill him, or Stringer Jack will kill us."

"Then we better get to it," the two men said, and drew their guns.

Before Clint reached the three rustlers, he knew they'd go for their guns. He tried to cut them off before they did it.

"Take it easy, boys," he called out. "Nobody needs to get hurt."

"What do we do?" Dutch Louie hissed at his two partners.

"Run!" Bill Williams said. "That's got to be Clint Adams."

"We have to fight," Orville Edwards said. "If we don't, Jack will kill us."

Clint reined his horse in, looked down at the three men.

"The easy way to do this is for you to lay down your guns."

Williams wanted to run, but if Louie and Orville survived, they'd mark him as a coward.

"Come on," Clint said. "Nobody has to die."

"Wrong!" a panicked Orville said. "You do."

He went for his gun . . .

Dixie Burr and Swift Bill went for their guns, and Piven quickly dove off his horse as they started to fire. He rolled on the ground, came up with his gun in his hand, and fired several times. The two rustlers went down after firing several shots of their own, and it was only when Piven stood that he realized he'd been hit.

* * *

Clint had no choice.

He drew, Eclipse keeping rock still beneath him, and fired three measured shots.

The three men drew their weapons and tried to fire quickly. Their shots went wild as Clint's shots flew straight and true. When the sounds of the shots faded away, all three rustlers were on the ground, dead.

Clint ejected his spent shells and replaced them before he dismounted and checked the bodies. Satisfied that they were dead, he checked the herd, made sure they were secure in the corral. He'd have to ride back to the stone arrow and meet up with the others. Then they'd return with shovels to bury these men, and any other rustlers who had ended up dead this day.

Hopefully, some of them had been taken alive.

Jim Doubt and Granville Stewart watched as the rest of the men strung up the two rustlers.

"You can't do this!" Red Mike yelled. His face was bloody from the beating Stewart had inflicted on him.

The other man, Brocky Gallagher, was barely conscious as they slipped the noose around his neck.

"Boss," Doubt said, "this ain't right. They gave us the name."

"Don't watch if you don't want to, Jim," Stewart said, "I'm makin' a statement here. Rustlers can't steal my cattle and get away with it."

"Yeah, but the law's out here," Doubt said. "Piven could ride up on us at any minute."

"I'm not hiding anything, Jim!" Stewart said. "I want

people to know this is what happens to rustlers if they come near the DHS."

"But . . . this is vigilantism."

"It sure is," Stewart said. "And we're going to track down the rest of the rustlers, and this Stringer Jack who's running them, and give them the same."

"Boss—" Doubt started, reaching for his boss's arm, but the man pulled away and rode up to the two mounted men with nooses around their necks. Their hands were tied behind their backs.

"Ready, boss," one of his men said.

"Do it!" Granville Stewart said.

Two men slapped the horses's rumps, and the two rustlers were swinging.

FORTY-TWO

When Clint arrived back at the stone arrow, he found Sheriff Nat Piven squatting there, picking up stones and tossing them into the distance. When he saw Clint, he stood up.

"I got three," Clint said.

"Dead?"

"Yes," Clint said, dismounting. "Didn't have a chance to question them, though."

"Well, I got two," Piven said, "same story. They gave me no choice, opened fire as soon as they saw my badge."

"That's what you get for wearing a target on your chest."

"Yeah, what's your excuse?"

Clint opened his canteen and took a drink, extended it to Piven, who shook his head. He'd already drunk from his own.

"We gotta get back to the bodies, get 'em buried," Piven said, "and tell Stewart where to pick up his cattle."

"Wonder where he and Doubt and their men have got to?" Clint asked.

"Well, I didn't see 'em, and neither did you, so they probably went ahead and followed that stone arrow of yours."

"I guess."

"In fact, that looks like them now," Piven said.

Clint turned and saw a bunch of riders in the distance, getting closer. When they came nearer, he saw both Granville Stewart and Jim Doubt at the head of the group.

They stood and waited for the men to reach them.

"How did you men do?" Stewart asked.

"Got five rustlers between us and found your cows," Piven said. "We can tell you where they are."

"We found the rest of the herd, and some horses, and dealt with two more," Stewart said.

Clint noticed that Jim Doubt did not look happy, and wasn't speaking.

"Dealt with?" Piven asked.

"They're dead."

"How many?"

"Two."

"So we got seven dead rustlers to bury. I'll need some of your men—"

"Forget it," Stewart said. "I need my men to bring back my cows. Besides, I'm not going to worry about burying some dead rustlers. Just tell me where my cows are."

"And you tell me where you left those two rustlers."

They exchanged directions, and Stewart and his men rode off, including the unhappy Jim Doubt.

"Did you notice Jim Doubt couldn't even look at us?" Clint asked.

"Yeah, I noticed," Piven said. "Maybe we should go and see what they did to those two rustlers."

They mounted up and followed their own stone arrow.

As Stewart, Doubt, and the other men rode off, Doubt said to his boss, "You shoulda told them about this Jack Stringer."

"Jack Stringer, Stringer Jack, whatever he wants to call himself," Stewart said, "is mine."

"Boss—"

"And if I find out you told Adams, or the sheriff, you're fired. You got that?"

"I got it."

"We're taking care of these rustlers and their leader ourselves. I'm not waiting for the law to put them away. I aim to send a message."

"Whatayou think's gonna happen when the sheriff finds those rustlers swingin' in the wind?"

"Nothin'," Stewart said. "He ain't gonna do a goddamned thing."

Doubt thought his boss was probably right, but it all still didn't sit well with him.

They followed Stewart's directions, crossed the Musselshell until they came to the two rustlers hanging from a tree.

"Damn it," Piven said. "Now I gotta arrest 'em."

"For what?" Clint asked. "Vigilantism? Good luck getting a jury to condemn them for that."

"You're probably right," Piven said. "Stewart will have the other ranchers behind him, probably all the businessmen, and the politicians."

"Not much you can do about that."

"I guess you're right."

"We better get back to town, come back out with some men as a burial detail and some buckboards."

"The undertaker's going to enjoy the extra business."

"Yeah," Piven said, "with more to come."

FORTY-THREE

It took a couple of days to get the cattle back where it belonged, and to bury the rustlers, which they did on the spot, instead of getting the undertaker involved.

Evie Loomis wrote up the story for the newspaper, after talking to the sheriff and Clint, and then going out to Granville Stewart's place to get his side of the story.

She got an earful from Stewart, who warned in print every rustler in the area to clear out. He said he and his men would take care of any rustler they found the same way they took care of the others. He didn't bother to mention that he was only responsible for the deaths of two of the seven rustlers. He pretty much made it sound like he'd killed them all.

For some reason, he and his men started to be called "Stewart's Stranglers," probably because of the men they had strung up.

It was clear that the rancher and his men were now a vigilante force.

* * *

Clint decided to stay around town awhile longer, in case Piven needed to face off with Stewart's Stranglers as well as rustlers.

He woke up in bed with Evie a few days after her big "Stranglers" story ran.

She had awakened first and was down between his legs, nibbling and licking at him, trying to wake him up.

"Mmm," she said, holding his thickening cock in her hand, "this part of you wakes up a lot easier and better than the rest."

"Good," he said, "then he can entertain you while I finish sleeping."

She kissed and licked the underside of his penis and said, "That's all right with me."

He closed his eyes. It was all right with him, too.

She sucked him until he was ready to burst, and then he flipped her onto her back and drove himself into her. He fucked her hard and fast while she held on for dear life until, finally, he finished with a loud yell, and she clung to him, holding him tightly until her own spasms subsided.

"I'm gonna miss waking up this way when you leave," she said into his ear.

He didn't respond. He didn't want her to ask him the question, because he'd been thinking about leaving any day now.

Things were not going the way Stringer Jack had planned.

His men had been rattled by the deaths of seven of their number. And although Jack had replaced those men with others, some of them had been picked off by the vigilantes and strung up. This made the remaining men even more nervous.

Still headquartered at Bates Point, Jack knew it was only a matter of time before the law or the vigilantes found them.

"Almost time to move on," Old Man James said.

"Not yet," Jack said.

"The men are nervous."

"Then they're actin' like old women," Jack said. "You ain' nervous, are ya, Old Man?"

"No," old Man James said, "but maybe at my age I just ain't got all that much to lose."

"You got your boys."

"Like I said," the older man said, "I ain't got all that much to lose."

Clint had breakfast with Evie. After that she went to the newspaper and he went to the sheriff's office.

"Glad to see you," Piven said.

"Why?"

"I just got word that Stringer Jack—real name Jack Stringer—and his men are out at Bates Point."

"And?"

"And Stewart and his men are headed out there," Piven explained.

"And what are we going to do?" Clint asked.

"We're gonna try to get out there first and take Stringer Jack into custody."

"And if we don't get there first?"

"Then I guess we'll have a big mess to clean up," Piven said. "You game?"

"Sure," Clint said, "I'm game. Why not?"

"Then let's go," Piven said, "but one thing."

"What?"

"Even though you can," the lawman said, "don't outrun me there."

FORTY-FOUR

Stringer Jack squatted in front of the fire. He was seething. Most of his men were gone. All he had left were Frank Hanson, Silas Nickerson, Paddy Rose, California Ed, along with Old Man James and his two boys.

Nickerson came riding into camp like his ass was on fire.

"Boss!"

"What?" Jack asked, knowing it was more bad news.

"A bunch of men are on the way here, 'bout five minutes out."

"Stewart?"

"Looks like him and his men."

Stringer Jack stood up, looked around.

"Get everybody together."

"Right."

Jack waited until all the man were gathered around him.

"Who's missin'?"

The men looked at each other.

"We're all here," Nickerson said.

"Then how did they find out we were there?" Jack asked.

"Maybe that ain't the important thing, Jack," Old Man James said.

"Then what is?"

"Gettin' out of here?" Old Man James said. "You and your men go."

"What about you and your boys?"

"We'll try and hold 'em here as long as we can."

"Why?"

"We live here," James said. "We'll tell them we ain't part of your gang."

"You think they'll believe that?"

"I hope so," James said, "but I ain't leavin' Bates Point. I like it here."

"Okay, then," Jack said. "Everybody get mounted."

"We runnin', Jack?" Frank Hanson asked.

"We're outnumbered, Frank," Jack said. "You wanna stay and fight?"

"What happened?" Paddy Rose asked. "We wuz supposed to hit it big hereabouts. What happened to that?"

"It went wrong, kid," Jack said. "We gotta get away and regroup. Now everybody . . . mount up!"

Stewart called his men to a halt.

"Doubt, take half the men and cross the Musselshell. If they run, you'll be able to cut them off."

"Right."

Doubt handpicked the men he wanted with him and

rode off. Granville Stewart took the remaining men and headed for Bates Point.

"How did you find out they're at Bates Point?" Clint asked.

"Got word from a fella named Charlie Batch. Said he was waterin' his mule in the Musselshell and saw some men and some cattle at Bates Point."

"And they didn't see him?"

"I guess not."

"And who else did he tell?" Clint asked.

"Well, I'm guessin' he sold the information to Stewart before he gave it to me for free."

"Great," Clint said. "So how do you want to play this?"

"How do you mean?"

"I mean, are we going to fire on the vigilantes?"

"I do that, I'm done in Judith Basin, and in these parts," Piven said. "But we may have to."

"I can do it," Clint said. "I've got nothing to lose around here."

"I guess we'll just have to handle that when the time comes," Piven said.

FORTY-FIVE

Granville Stewart and his men rode into Bates Point with their guns out. Old Man James and his sons were immediately covered.

"Drop 'em!" Stewart shouted.

"Let 'em drop, boys," Old Man James said. "These here are Stewart's Stranglers. We don't wanna give them a reason to string us up."

His sons both dropped their rifles to the ground.

"What do you want here, Stewart?"

"You know what I want, James," Stewart said. "Stringer Jack and his men were holed up here. Where are they now?"

"Don't know what you're talkin' about."

"We can see all these tracks, old man."

"Then track 'em."

Stewart pointed to one of James's sons.

"String him up," he ordered.

Two men dismounted, ran to the young man, and

grabbed his arms. One of them had a rope and they started dragging him to a tree.

"Pa! Pa!"

The older man tried to hold off, but in the end he said, "Okay. Okay."

The two men stopped and looked at their boss. Stewart held his hand up.

"They only left about ten minutes ago," he said. "They're crossin' the river."

Stewart knew they were running right into Jim Doubt and the other men, but he needed to get there so that his men would outnumber the rustlers.

"Three of you stay here," Stewart said, "and string up the two boys."

"Hey! I told you what you wanna know!" the old man said.

"I've got to make an example, James," Stewart said.

"You sonofa—" The old man started to go for his fallen rifle, but Stewart yelled, "Don't!"

"Why not?" Old Man James said. "You're gonna hang me anyway."

The old man started to go for the rifle. Granville Stewart drew his gun.

"Hold it, both of you!"

All eyes went to the speaker, Clint Adams.

"This is none of your business, Adams. Yours neither, Sheriff."

"You can't let him hang my boys, Sheriff," James shouted. "They ain't done nothin'."

"That's probably not true, Mr. James, but you're right. I can't let them be hung." He turned to Stewart. "Call your men off, Granville."

Stewart didn't speak.

"Boss," one of the men asked.

"You can't do anything, Sheriff," Stewart said. "The town supports the vigilantes. You'll be out of a job if you harm one of us."

"I won't," Clint said. "I don't have a job to worry about. I'll kill the first man who tries to harm one of these men."

Stewart gave Clint a hard look. He pointed at the three men.

"Even if they're not rustlers, at the very least they gave shelter to the rustlers."

"Last I heard," Clint said, "that's not a hangin' offense."

Stewart held Clint's eyes as long as he could, then said to his men, "Let him go."

Clint looked around, didn't see Jim Doubt, and realized that not all of Stewart's men were there.

"Where are the rest of your men?" he demanded.

At that moment they heard shots in the distance.

"That'd be the rest of my men taking care of the rest of the rustlers."

Clint looked at Piven. There was nothing they could do. They'd never get there in time, and if they did, they'd be hopelessly outnumbered.

"Now, Sheriff," Stewart said, "if you'll allow us to do our job."

Stewart waved at his men and rode off in the direction of the river. His men followed, the two on foot rushing to their horses.

"Damn it," Piven said.

"Stewart's Stranglers," Clint said. "The ones they don't shoot, they'll hang."

"And the ones that get away, they continue to hunt."

"You can't do anything, Nat," Clint said. "You can't fight vigilantism alone, and I can't stay any longer to help you."

"I know that," Piven said. "Maybe I'll just keep giving the newspaper something to write about."

"That'd be the way to do it, I guess."

"You boys get inside," Old Man James said. Then he and the boys started to pick up their guns.

"Uh-uh, old man," Piven said, producing his gun. "I've got to have somethin' to show for my efforts. All three of you mount up. You're under arrest."

Clint holstered his gun. Piven had this part under control. Granville Stewart would end up getting his way, like most men as rich as he was did. Clint could have left the area immediately. There was nothing in his hotel room he couldn't do without. But in the end he decided to ride back with Piven, to make sure he got the three outlaws—and himself—there safely.

"You comin' back with me?" Piven asked.

"Yeah," Clint said. "Get 'em mounted. I'll help you get them back. Might as well say good-bye to Evie before I leave."

"I'm afraid the way this is turnin' out wasn't really worth you comin here," Piven said. "Sorry, Clint. But I sure am glad you came."

"We did what we could, Nat," Clint told him. "That's all anybody can ever do."

"Yeah," Piven said, "I'll tell that to Evie and let her put it in her newspaper."

Watch for

HUNT FOR THE WHITE WOLF

356th novel in the exciting GUNSMITH series
from Jove

Coming in August!